Alec Birri served thirty years with the UK Armed Forces. He commanded an operational unit that experimented in new military capabilities classified at the highest level (Top Secret Strap 3) and it is this that forms the basis of his novels.

Although semi-autobiographical, for national security and personal liberty reasons, the events and individuals portrayed have to be fiction, but are still nonetheless in keeping with his experiences.

www.alecbirri.com

CONDITION

BOOK ONE

ALEC BIRRI

Matador
9 Priory Business Park,
Wistow Road, Kibworth Beauchamp,
Leicestershire. LE8 0RX
Tel: (+44) 116 279 2299
Fax: (+44) 116 279 2277
Email: books@troubador.co.uk
Web: www.troubador.co.uk/matador

ISBN 978 1785899 683

British Library Cataloguing in Publication Data.
A catalogue record for this book is available from the British Library.

Typeset in 11pt Aldine by Troubador Publishing Ltd, Leicester, UK

Matador is an imprint of Troubador Publishing Ltd

To My Mother.

PROLOGUE

The aircraft came to a halt and the fire spread. The pilot just had time to acknowledge he'd survived when smoke reminded him to get out – fast. He motioned to release the restraint harness but couldn't and, when he looked down to take a second attempt, realised why – a bone was protruding through the skin of his right forearm.

He tried using his left hand instead, but couldn't move that either. Attempts to lift his right leg and then his left confirmed he'd been trapped by a combination of injury and the aircraft's wrecked systems and controls.

Between the flames he could see movement outside – blue flashing lights and people running around, so his extraction was only a matter of time. He forced himself to remain calm and even paused to consider the pointless irony of surviving a crash only to die afterwards.

That changed when fire reached bare flesh for the first time. His flight suit and gloves were designed to be fire-retardant but the exposed wrist of his right arm wasn't, and he couldn't help but cry out at the acid-like contact.

'Get me out! Get me out!' he screamed.

A gentle breeze through shattered glass kept most of the smoke away from his face, so he could make the urgency of the situation clear, but, along with plastics, metals, fluids, flesh, and bone, the steady supply of oxygen was all the fire needed too.

The skin around his wrist reddened, blistered, and peeled. He wanted to pass out with the pain, but its persistence ensured he continued to witness the torture.

Further flames erupted and began cutting through his whole arm. The protection afforded by the glove and sleeve soon burnt away causing a torment of fizzing and popping flesh to make him scream all the more.

He clenched a fist but the brittle skin split, exposing the tendons and veins underneath. The pain did eventually ease somewhat, but only because receptors in the epidermis had now burnt away.

He could clearly see his right hand and arm being consumed. What he couldn't see was the fire making its way up and around the seat to his whole body. Inch by inch, the flames first singed and then penetrated his clothing before attacking the flesh beneath. The breeze kept his head clear for now, but it was only a matter of time.

He became aware of a strange acceptance and his panic subsided with it. He looked towards the broken window, where the frantic efforts to save him could still be seen. There were other things too – the sun, clouds, and trees in the distance. He could even see grass next to his head, which made him realise both he and the cockpit must be lying on one side.

His head was so close, the individual blades stood out and he marvelled at how calming grass could be.

Small wild flowers nestled within and a lone bumble bee arrived for a moment to bounce its way between. All this with a raging inferno just feet away. He had never really appreciated nature before and wondered why he did now.

There was laughter amongst the shouts of the rescuers. Had they saved him? Was he out? Were they congratulating themselves on a job well done? He realised the laughter was actually that of his daughter, giggling and playing amongst them. Why? What on earth had possessed his wife to think that that'd be safe? He glanced above the instrument panel and just had time to smile before their photograph was reduced to ash.

He looked outside again, and they smiled back. It was the perfect summer's day, but for some inexplicable reason his wife had decided it would be a good idea to have a barbecue right next to a burning aircraft. He tried talking to her about it, but nothing came out. Something in his throat stopped him. A sensation of melting around his face and neck caused him to closed his eyes. He could still see his family, though, and they beckoned him to join them.

The smell of roasting meat made him salivate.

PART ONE

CHAPTER ONE

'Come on, Danny – wake up!'

'Wake up, Dad.' It was his daughter's voice.

Someone took hold of his hand. For a second he thought both his wife and daughter must be in the aircraft with him, but accepted the nonsense of that. No, he was somewhere much quieter.

'Dad, can you hear me?'

Sounded more like his wife. His left hand was being caressed. He decided to chance opening his eyes. Not in the aircraft any more. Somewhere less mechanical and, judging by the smell, much less inviting than a barbecue in the sun.

'Dad, do you recognise me?'

He squinted at the shock of blonde hair. It never ceased to amaze him how much Claire looked like their daughter. Or was it the other way around? She didn't seem to be with her, though.

'Where's Lucy?' he croaked.

'No, Dan… It's me, Claire.'

He focussed on his wife and tried to smile.

'Boy, are you a sight for sore eyes. Where am I?'

He scanned the room before answering his own

question. 'A hospital. How did I get here? How did I get out of the crash?'

'Try not to stress yourself, you're still very weak.'

He glanced down and, as expected, his right hand and arm were bandaged. He winced at the memory of seeing the back of his hand with the flesh removed. By comparison, his left arm and hand were bare, but displaying a disturbing loss of muscle mass. What he assumed to be skin grafts made him feel sick. It hurt to move his fingers too – crush injuries from the aircraft being on its side, he decided. Dan recalled the sensation of his face and neck melting.

'I need a mirror.'

Claire rummaged through her handbag, opened a compact, and passed it to him. Dan raised it to his eyes.

He was expecting the worst, but it still came as a shock. Even with bandages covering most of his head, his face did indeed look as if it had melted.

Loose, wrinkled, and ugly skin now hung where much firmer flesh used to be – more like that of an old man, rather than his thirty-six years. He closed his eyes and tried to hold back tears, but they came anyway.

'It's okay; everything is okay. You're safe now.'

'How can you even look at me like this?' he sobbed.

'It's okay. Everything is going to be okay.'

Claire squeezed his hand and he tried to squeeze hers back, but it hurt too much. She was smiling at him. His face didn't seem to bother her; or if it did, she was good at hiding it.

'You're still a looker,' she gently mocked.

'And you're a liar,' he joined in. Dan became serious. 'I don't want Lucy seeing me like this.'

'Too late – we've both been to see you and many times – she's your daughter and doesn't care how you look.'

Dan wasn't convinced, and pondered the years of plastic surgery he would have to endure, and how he would look at the end of it. 'How long have I been here?'

'About six months.'

'*Six months*? I've been unconscious for six months?'

Dan was surprised, but it explained why only his right arm and head were still in plaster and bandages – he imagined there wouldn't have been much of him that wasn't at some stage. At least he hadn't had to endure consciousness through all of that. He sharpened up.

'Football! What happened in the football?'

Claire looked at him blankly.

'We're hosting the World Cup this year – what's the date? Have I missed it?'

Claire started to reply, but Dan stopped her.

'Shush! Don't say anything. I don't want to know how far England got, just in case I have.'

He looked around the room for something to confirm the date, but other than the clock next to his bed saying it was just after twenty-five past eight in the evening, there was nothing.

'It's the sixteenth of August.'

'Bugger,' Dan exclaimed, despondently. 'I've just missed it – make sure no one tells me any of the results!'

Claire kissed him on the forehead. 'I'm sure you've no need to worry.'

There was a knock on the door and a man entered. He smiled at Claire, which annoyed Dan for some reason.

'Awake, I see. Good morning. Do you know who I am?'

Dan shook his head.

'My name's Doctor Adams. How are we today?'

'Okay, I suppose,' Dan answered limply. He knew he was just feeling sorry for himself, but still decided the doctor wasn't someone he would naturally warm to – probably because most women would.

The doctor took Dan's temperature and pulse, and then checked over the bandages. 'I think some of these dressings can come off today. Mind if I ask you a few questions?'

'I suppose not,' Dan replied. He was starting to sound pathetic so tried perking up. 'I mean, yeah, sure.'

'What's your name?'

'Winston Churchill.'

Claire told him to take it seriously.

'At least I've still got my sense of humour,' Dan mumbled.

'With the emphasis on "my", as nobody else has it,' Claire shot back.

Her look of mock indignation told Dan she was actually relieved to see something of his old self. He turned back to the doctor.

'Squadron Leader Daniel Stewart.'

'And how old are you?'

'Thirty-six.'

'What year is it?'

'1966 – sixteenth of August apparently.' He flashed a wink at Claire.

The questions kept coming. 'Who's the prime minister?'

'Harold Wilson – or at least he was six months ago.'

'Who won the World Cup?'

'Don't tell me!' Dan put his hands over his ears, but pain forced him to drop them again.

Claire made a request. 'Do you think it might be possible to get a recording of the matches?'

Doctor Adams appeared to hesitate before replying, 'I should think so.' He turned back to his patient. 'Squadron Leader Stewart, do you remember the accident?'

Dan knew his injuries warranted all these questions, but he had to be careful with his next answer – as a military pilot he often dealt with sensitive and classified information and, as qualified as the doctor was, he probably didn't have the necessary clearances. Especially as this particular mission... He stopped himself mid-thought when it occurred to him he couldn't recall anything about it. He pondered the accident carefully. Nope, nothing – just the post-crash fire.

'I... can... remember...,' he said, before raising his right arm, 'incredible pain.' He winced at the recollection of flesh being peeled away layer by layer. He looked towards the room's window, where the sun could just be made out through some clouds. 'Trees... grass...

flowers.' He turned back to Claire and the doctor. 'And a bumble bee.' He realised how silly he must sound and his mood dropped again.

Doctor Adams became sympathetic. 'Squadron Leader Stewart – may I call you Dan?'

Dan nodded.

'Nobody goes through a trauma like yours without being affected psychologically in some way. You didn't just suffer burns and a fracture – you have a head injury too. You might look fine, but it's what's going on inside that counts. Are you aware of the memory difficulties you're having?'

Dan nodded, reluctantly.

'That's good. Recognition of the problem is an important step. You've only just woken up, so I think we should give you a day or so and then look at your medication to see if there's anything that can be done to help. In the meantime, you need to get moving so I'll arrange for some physiotherapy.'

He made a couple of notes on the chart at the end of the bed, before asking: 'Do you have any questions for me?'

Dan had a million buzzing around somewhere in his battered brain, but decided just to ask what his prognosis was.

'Well, if you respond to the physio and your memory starts to recover, then you could be back to normal in as little as three months.'

'Back to flying, you mean?' Dan asked, nervously.

Doctor Adams glanced at Claire. 'Let's just take one

step at a time.' With that, he placed his pen back into his coat pocket and left the room.

'That's my career over then. May as well give up now,' Dan muttered to himself pitifully.

'Now come on, don't be like that – you could have died.' Claire sat on the edge of the bed, placed his left arm on her lap, and massaged it.

It was a loving gesture and yet at the same time she seemed distant. Caring, but strangely cold. Dan wanted her to be all over him with emotion and wondered why she wasn't. 'You heard him,' he moaned. 'One step at a time. That's as good as saying: forget it, mate.'

Claire chuckled. 'You're as stubborn as a mule. If I know you, you'll be running around chasing nurses in no time!' He found her words patronising.

If her intention was to boost his morale, it didn't work. Dan wanted to bring her mood down to his. 'It wouldn't bother you if I did, would it?'

She stopped massaging his arm. Dan knew he would end up regretting his next question, but asked it anyway. 'Do you think he's good-looking?'

Claire got off the bed. 'Dan, you are the most important person in my life and nothing else matters more to me right now than seeing you get better.'

He firmed his attitude. 'You didn't answer my question – do you think Doctor Adams is good-looking?'

'I'll say!' The door opened and in walked a nurse, answering the question. She was pushing a small trolley in front of her and the contents made it clear it was time to remove Dan's dressings. 'He's a dreamboat!' She smiled at the two of them and a couple of smiles were forced back. 'Have I come at a bad time?'

'No,' they both replied in unison.

'I have to go anyway,' Claire blurted out.

She kissed Dan goodbye, which he noticed wasn't quite full on the lips. She paused on the way out.

'I'll be in again, tomorrow. Please try not to fret – there really is nothing to worry about.'

She blew a kiss in Dan's direction and left.

'She seems nice.'

'Mmmm?'

'Your daughter – she seems very nice.'

Dan was offended. 'She's my wife,' he replied, irritated. 'Do I really look that old?'

The nurse blushed and tried talking her way out of it. 'No, what I mean is, er, you're a very lucky…'

He chose to end her suffering. 'It's okay, I know I must be a terrible sight.'

'No, not at all.'

Dan could see she was still uncomfortable, so forced a further smile. 'You're another good liar,' he tried to joke.

She composed herself. 'Anyway, my name's Tracy and I've come to remove your dressings. All right?'

'Be my guest.'

She began by checking the existing bandages as Doctor Adams had previously, giving Dan the opportunity to study her too. His conclusions couldn't have been more different, only he didn't so much as warm to her as 'heat'.

It wasn't that Tracy was particularly attractive – in fact, she was a bit of a frump if Dan was to be honest. No, it was something he'd always had a weakness for in women – her large breasts. Her large breasts – in a uniform. He found himself staring, so pretended to look out of the window.

Tracy turned away to prepare her instruments on the trolley, and he looked back. Dan confirmed her frumpiness: she was about five feet tall, flat shoes, dark hair tied up in a tight bun under the obligatory nurse's hat, and carrying a lot of excess weight. He guessed she was in her late twenties, but a lack of style and homely appearance made her look much older.

She was probably wearing the same-sized uniform she'd always worn, which meant it was now figure-hugging. Ordinarily, this would appeal to Dan, but it unfortunately outlined a series of unattractive rolls of flesh on her back, which progressively became larger as they descended, with the last of them not quite merging with her bottom. *Very Rubensesque*, he thought.

Dan was wondering how much weight she would have to lose to even start to look sexy in that uniform, when Tracy turned to one side and continued her preparations. He looked out of the window again to avoid eye contact, before turning back to resume his ruminations. The objects of his fascination were now outlined from the side.

God, they're magnificent, he thought and hoped he hadn't said it out loud.

Something inside Dan began to stir. He couldn't

take his eyes off them and started to feel guilty; he was a happily married man after all. He tried thinking less sexual thoughts. Anatomically speaking, they were no different to the ugly rolls of flesh on her back. They even seemed to start from there – at the very top, running around and under each armpit before spilling into and over what must have been one of the largest bras ever made. He knew full well that without this very necessary device, her two huge breasts would just hang pendulously in front of him. Dan swallowed. Hard.

'Right then. I think that's everything. Shall we start with your arm, or would you like a bed bath first?'

Tracy turned sharply back towards him, causing her chest to swing one way and then the other, before settling back in front in a decreasing series of heaves. Dan's penis became erect.

'My arm!' he blustered. 'My arm, please.'

Dan blushed and he tried to think of something else. Tracy gave him a look that he often got from his wife, and it made him feel just as uncomfortable – like a naughty boy caught doing something he shouldn't. Tracy selected a pair of surgical scissors and began cutting the old bandage down the length of his arm.

Dan looked down at the bed covers and was relieved to see they were thick enough to cover his embarrassment, which was still firmly pointing towards his navel. 'At least something still works,' he mumbled under his breath.

'Sorry?' Tracy asked.

'Nothing, er, did you watch the football?' He

admonished himself for not making less risky small talk. Fortunately for him, she wasn't a fan.

'Nah, not really my thing. We can talk about it if you want to, though?'

'No, that's okay,' Dan replied, somewhat relieved. 'It's just that I missed the World Cup, so…' His voice trailed away as he realised Tracy was about to expose his right hand for the first time.

She sensed the concern. 'You can look away if you want – or keep looking at me.'

Tracy smiled and Dan blushed again. Was she flirting with him? Either way, his ego reinflated. 'No, that's okay, I want to see it.' Dan didn't, but thought he would be more of a man if he did.

Tracy removed the remaining bandage, which exposed the plaster cast sleeve and a thin pad covering the back of his hand. It clung to what was underneath and Dan could already see it wasn't exactly thick skin. His erection became less of an issue. Taking a pair of forceps, Tracy gripped a corner of the pad and began lifting it away. The movement reminded Dan of his skin peeling in the fire and his stomach lurched.

'Do you want me to stop?'

'No,' Dan responded. 'Keep going.' The pad came away – to his horror, the tendons and veins were still exposed. 'My God, it hasn't healed at all,' he blurted out. A lump came to his throat and his eyes watered.

'What are you talking about? It's doing really well. Still a bit red, I grant you, but well on the mend.'

'But there isn't any flesh!'

'Of course there is,' Tracy said. 'Apart from the colour, it looks exactly the same as your other hand – look.'

Dan lifted his left arm and brought the two together. He compared the backs of both. Sure enough, other than his right hand being a bit pinker, they were almost identical. 'It's like all the muscle and fat's gone,' he said.

'Sounds like a good excuse to eat lots of cake, to me.' Tracy slapped one of her ample hips.

'I can see you're something of an expert in that department.'

'Oi! Do you want me to finish or what?'

Dan tried being more of the 'officer and a gentleman' he was supposed to be. 'Sorry, Tracy, what I mean to say is: I think you have a very attractive figure.'

'Yes,' she purred, taking a deep breath and expanding her chest to its largest possible size, 'I know you do.'

There was no doubt about it; under normal circumstances Dan would find her a very welcome distraction – but not right now. He studied his withered left arm and shivered. 'Tracy, I want to see what the rest of me looks like. Do you think you could help me to sit up?'

'Of course I can.' She put down the forceps and moved to his opposite side. 'I'm just going to shift you up the bed a bit first.'

He went to grip the frame with his left hand but weakness and pain thwarted him. 'Might be an idea to get some help.'

'Nonsense,' Tracy said, dismissing the idea. 'I'm stronger than I look.'

Dan very much doubted that. Before the crash he'd been a good thirteen stone and, even given six months of muscle wastage in a coma, he must still have been at least eleven. She tucked her right arm under his back, her left under his legs, and pulled him up the bed as if he were a small child.

'My God,' Dan said in disbelief. 'You weren't joking. Remind me not to upset you.'

Tracy winked and reached for the remote control. The top third of the bed started to rise. Dan readied himself for some back pain but, to his relief, none came.

'High enough?'

He nodded. Tracy put down the remote and, after adjusting his pillows, pulled back the covers. The striped pyjamas Dan was wearing only seemed to emphasise the impression of a concentration camp victim – he appeared to be little more than a skeleton wrapped in skin. About six stone at most. No wonder she managed to move him so easily.

Shocked by his appearance, Dan reached forward with his left hand and, despite the pain, pulled back a leg of his pyjamas. Like his arm and hands, the skin on his leg and foot was impossibly thin. He could see straight through to the sinews, blood vessels, veins, and even the bones within. Dan continued to pull the pyjama leg back to reveal a knee twice the width of his calf. He closed his eyes and tried not to be sick.

'Are you okay?'

Dan didn't answer. He had expected his flesh to be damaged by the fire, but never realised just how much muscle, fat, and other tissue would be consumed too. It was a miracle he was even alive. He put his head down and wished he was dead. Why wasn't he? Tears flowed.

'Now come on, no feeling sorry for yourself.' Tracy plainly thought the 'be a man' approach was best at times like this. 'All you need is exercise and plenty of pies.'

She put both hands on her belly and puffed out her cheeks. Dan coughed with laughter at the ridiculous pose.

'Why can't you just leave me alone to die in peace?' He was chuckling and crying at the same time.

'Not allowed to, I'm afraid. Got to at least finish removing your dressings first.'

Dan couldn't take it all in. Talk about a rollercoaster of emotions. Might all be in a day's work to Tracy, but this was very much new territory for him. He pulled himself together.

'Tracy, I know you're only trying to help, but right now I just want to feel sorry for myself. Okay?'

'Suit yourself.' She seemed only slightly offended. 'Okay to finish your dressings?'

Dan forced yet another smile and nodded. Tracy removed the last of the bandages in silence while Dan did a lot of thinking. He decided that as long as there was hope, everything would be okay. He needed to get out of bed for a start. A bit of physio, some serious exercise, weights in the gym, and one hell of a lot of food. He grinned.

'What's so funny?' Tracy asked.

'I was just thinking about your cakes and pies.'

'Hey! Nothing wrong with cakes and pies. Never did me any harm.' She shot an open palm towards his mouth. 'Don't even think about making another rude comment.'

'I wasn't going to,' he lied. 'You know I fancy you like mad.'

'No, you don't. You fancy these.' She placed her hands under her breasts and juggled each one up and down for a second.

The covers were still at the foot of the bed, so there was nothing to stop another unwanted erection appearing through the fly of Dan's pyjamas. Mortified, he rushed to cover it.

Grinning like a Cheshire cat, Tracy took hold of the bedclothes and pulled them back up to his chest. 'Told you,' she purred, and kissed him on the forehead. 'I think we'll leave the bed bath till next time. Don't you?'

Dan nodded sheepishly. Still grinning, Tracy turned to her trolley and prepared to leave.

'The doctor will be in, but I think you'll be fine. Is there anything else I can do for you?' She paused before adding: 'Within reason.'

Dan shook his head.

'Right then. I'll be off. Just press the buzzer by your bed if you change your mind.'

She turned to leave, pushing the trolley in front of her. Dan looked at her retreating form and did indeed change his mind – a pair of stiletto heels and she'd be perfect. Tracy was about to close the door when Dan called her back.

'What now?' she asked in fake exasperation.

'Sorry, Tracy, but something's been bugging me about the dressings and this plaster cast.'

'What about them?'

'Well, why are they so late in coming off compared to my other injuries? I mean, I've been here for six months.'

'I don't know anything about any other injuries,' Tracy admitted. 'But these came off because they were due to.' She strode over to the foot of the bed, picked up his chart and studied it. 'Hmmm. You might have been here for six months, but your treatment only started on the second of August – that means your accident was two weeks ago.'

CHAPTER TWO

'Good afternoon, Squadron Leader.'

Dan sensed a degree of mockery in the words. There was – his brother had entered the room. Dan groaned as Brian ignored any pleasantries and launched straight into his opinion on one of the few interests they shared.

'Did you see the jugs on *that*?'

Brian must have passed Tracy in the corridor. Dan knew he could be guilty of behaving like an adolescent sometimes, but his brother revelled in it.

'Jeezus!' he continued. 'What I wouldn't give to get my hands on *those*!'

Dan moved from irritation to annoyance. 'It may have escaped your notice, but I have more important things on my mind at the moment.' Dan knew it wouldn't stop Brian, but he had to say something.

'Never mind that – what a woman! Forget all this medical nonsense. What you need is a daily dose of those in your face – you'll be out of here in no time!'

Anybody else and Dan might have laughed, but he didn't get on with his brother at the best of times. He looked out of the window. 'Brian, please don't take this the wrong way, but I just want to be alone right now.'

'Who's Brian?'

Dan turned back to his brother and found himself looking at Doctor Adams.

'Er, he's my brother.' Dan looked past the doctor to see if Brian was elsewhere in the room. He wasn't. 'I could have sworn you were...'

'Interesting.' The doctor observed Dan as if he were a culture in a Petri dish. 'Do I look like your brother?'

'No,' Dan replied, becoming irritated for a different reason this time. He knew the doctor was only doing his job, but he seemed to enjoy it too much.

'And is your brother in the room now?'

'Of course not.'

'So what can be concluded from this?'

Dan now felt like a first-year medical student looking into said Petri dish. 'That he just walked out?'

Adams waited.

'Hallucinating. I was hallucinating.'

'Very good.'

'Very good? It's *good* that I'm hallucinating?'

'No, it's good that you *acknowledge* you were hallucinating.'

That was it. Dan had had enough. 'Right then. Now it's my turn – I've got some questions for *you*.' He raised his right arm. 'What can be concluded from *this*?'

Adams studied the limb then Dan's head. 'I conclude the burn to the back of your hand and the cuts and bruises on your head have healed.'

The doctor seemed to be toying with him. 'What

about the fact that I only sustained those injuries two weeks ago?'

'Then I would say you either remember how you came by them or, given the hallucination just now, it's more likely you have knowledge of what's on the chart at the end of your bed.'

If the doctor was hiding anything, he was playing it cool.

'So let me get this right,' Dan continued. 'Six months ago, I arrived here barely alive and in need of a medical miracle, only to suffer some kind of accident in *your* care. Is that right?'

Adams thought for a second before replying. 'That's correct.'

Dan became angry. 'Unbelievable. I nearly die in an aircraft crash, only to suffer yet *more* injuries at the hands of your incompetent staff! What have you got to say about that? What kind of joke is this place? You couldn't make it up. It's the most outrageous thing I've ever heard. I'm going to have to take some serious legal advice about this. You'd better get yourself a good lawyer, because you're going to need...'

Dan's chest tightened. He couldn't breathe. He grasped at his throat. Eyes and mouth wide open, he extended his right hand to the doctor. Adams just looked at him. Brian reappeared and just looked at him. The room went black and Dan passed out.

Dan opened his eyes. He didn't know how long he'd been out for, but sensed it wasn't long.

'Drink this,' he heard a voice say.

He reached out to take the glass, but stopped when he realised who was offering it. 'Get away from me.'

'I'm sorry?'

'I said, get away from me.'

Adams did as he was told.

'Stay there.' Dan kept his eyes on the doctor and reached for the buzzer. He pressed it repeatedly. 'You tried to kill me.'

'Don't be so ridiculous.'

'You could see I couldn't breathe and yet you did nothing.'

'I think you'll find there is a difference.'

'Don't give me that crap – I'm on to you.'

Tracy burst in. 'Okay, where's the fire?'

'Tracy, thank God, tell me what's in that glass.'

'What?'

'I need to know what's in that glass.'

Her eyes flitted back and forth between the two men. 'What's going on?'

'Nothing – if there's just water in that glass.' Dan tried sounding plausible.

The doctor offered the tumbler to Tracy. She raised it to the window for a better view and then gave it a sniff. 'Looks like water to me.'

'Then the doctor won't mind if you drink it, will he?' Dan glared at him.

Adams shrugged. Tracy took a couple of sips before shrugging too. Dan buried his face in his hands and broke down.

'What's going on? I don't understand,' he wailed.

Tracy rushed to console him like a mother hen.

Adams remained impassive as he spoke. 'Amnesia, hallucinations, and now, paranoia. The drug treatment must be restarted immediately.'

'I'm not taking anything,' Dan protested. 'Especially from you.'

'Shhh… calm yourself,' Tracy soothed.

She already had an arm around his shoulders, so it was easy for Dan to drop his head to her chest – which he did. The comforting non-sexual warmth was surprising and made him realise Brian – or, rather, his hallucination – was right, just not in the way he or it meant. Dan stopped feeling so sorry for himself.

'Dan?' Adams had adopted a sympathetic tone again.

What was he scheming now? Dan thought he would make a good Bond villain.

'What if you were to revisit the scene of the accident?'

Dan took his head off Tracy's chest. 'You mean go back to where the aircraft crashed?'

Adams paused before answering. 'No, I mean the accident you had here.'

'But I've been unconscious for six months.'

Adams glanced at Tracy. 'No, you haven't.'

Dan dropped his head back towards the pillows, so Tracy withdrew her arm. He stared at the wall opposite. 'There's something seriously wrong with me, isn't there?'

The two medical professionals nodded. Dan felt nothing. It was as if emotions were something that could be used up and he was now on empty.

'Take me there,' he said.

The doctor picked up Dan's chart and made an entry. 'Could you arrange that please, Tracy?' He looked at his watch. 'It's one o'clock – you may as well take the squadron leader for lunch at the same time. I'll meet you both there shortly.'

He left the room and Tracy walked over to a hoist in the corner. 'Do me a favour, Dan, press your buzzer – we're going to need some help.'

Dan turned to his left and did as he was told. The bedside clock caught his eye. It still read eight-twenty-six in the evening. 'Even that's broken,' he muttered.

'God, I hope not. I don't mind shifting you up the bed on my own, but I draw the line at lifting you out of it.'

'No, I meant the clock – it's broken.'

Tracy seemed puzzled, and was about to say something when the door opened. 'Ah, Mike, can you give me a hand?'

Within a few minutes, the two nurses had Dan up and into a wheelchair.

'Do you want a blanket for your knees?' Tracy asked.

Dan shook his head.

'Are you sure? We don't want to risk making a spectacle of ourselves again, do we?' She nodded towards his groin. Mike put a hand over his mouth and left the room. Laughter trailed away down the corridor.

'You've told everyone, haven't you?'

'No,' Tracy said with fake innocence. 'I've only mentioned it twice – once to Mike and once to the rest of the nursing staff.'

'God, I hate you.'

'No, you don't, and we both know why.' Breasts pressed against the back of Dan's neck as she kissed the top of his head.

Tracy pushed Dan out into the corridor and parked him there. He found himself looking into the room opposite. The movement of the wheelchair caught the occupant's eye who took hold of a handle above his bed to get a better view.

His arm was bare, and straight away Dan noticed injuries similar to his own – heavy scarring with much of the flesh and muscle either damaged or wasted. Dan guessed they were about the same age, but burns to the other man's face made him look much older.

The occupant presented a toothless smile. Dan ran his tongue over his own teeth to make sure they were still there. The poor guy was missing a leg too, which made Dan feel both sorry for his neighbour and better for himself at the same time. A pang of guilt ensured Dan understood there were still people in this world worse off than him.

Tracy pushed her patient down the corridor. They approached a couple of hospital porters, who grinned at them both before bursting into fits of laughter as they passed.

Dan sighed. 'I suppose being the hospital joke is part of my treatment?'

Tracy chuckled. 'You make me laugh – that's a good thing.'

'Well, as long as I'm still of some service to society.'

Tracy chuckled again. 'See? It's important for a man to make a woman laugh. Much more attractive than looks alone.'

He took it as a compliment, but the jury would have to be out on her statement until after the plastic surgery. A porter approached with a patient in another wheelchair and Tracy stopped to talk to him. Dan thought it only polite to pass the time of day with his charge.

'Good afternoon.' No acknowledgement. 'Lovely day.' Dan knew he wasn't trying. *God, I'm an awful person*, he thought.

The woman in the wheelchair was wearing a robe with a hood that covered her face, and the only reason Dan assumed she was female was because of its feminine design and colour – bright pink.

He couldn't see her hands either, but judging by her small size and posture assumed her to be old and frail. Dan leaned forward to see if he could catch her eye, when she spoke.

'Have you seen my mummy?'

She was a little girl! Dan still couldn't see her face, but guessed she was about his daughter's age.

'No, I haven't I'm afraid. What's her name?'

'She said she would come back for me, but she didn't.'

A lump came to Dan's throat. Whatever had happened to or was wrong with this poor child, he knew there was nothing he could do and he felt helpless – which, of course, he was. He couldn't even help himself.

A doll fell to the floor. With a great deal of effort and considerable pain Dan picked it up.

A tiny hand reached out from under the robe. Dan's blood ran cold – it had been burnt almost to a crisp. No dressings, bandages – or flesh. Just the same sickening sight of exposed veins, tendons, and scarring. No wonder she didn't want to look at him. She took the doll and held it close to her. Tracy and the porter finished their conversation and continued on their respective ways.

'Who was that?' Dan asked. 'She wanted to know if I'd seen her mother.'

'You mean Alice?' Tracy seemed surprised by his interest. 'Very sad story, I'm afraid, and patient confidentiality forbids me from telling you anything – it's private.'

Dan wasn't impressed. 'Hmmm. Whereas broadcasting the confidentiality of *my* privates across the hospital would appear to be a medical necessity.'

Tracy turned to face him. 'It's not a joke, Dan – her mother's dead.'

Dan was embarrassed. 'Sorry,' he said meekly. 'That's awful. Poor thing – what's going to happen to her?'

Tracy didn't respond and continued to push him down the corridor. Dan guessed Alice must have been involved in a car accident or something, during which her mother had died; but not before making a promise she could never keep. He absent-mindedly placed a hand against his bottom lip while trying not to think of his own daughter in the same situation. He dropped it again when he realised it looked a lot like Alice's.

He brought his hand back up. 'Tracy?'

'Yes, my sweet?'

'Is this a specialist burns unit?'

'Not particularly, why?'

'It's just that my hand looks almost exactly like Alice's.'

'Stop being nosey about Alice.'

'I'm not – the chap in the room opposite mine has similar injuries to me, and so does Alice.'

'Everybody here has been through the mill one way or another, so there are bound to be some common ailments.'

'I suppose so,' Dan replied, not entirely convinced. They passed a sign pointing to a canteen and kept on going. 'I thought we were going to have lunch?' Dan realised he was hungry and, Lord knows, he needed to eat.

'We are, but it's a lovely summer's day so everyone's outside.'

They rounded a corner and passed through a glass conservatory. The sun streamed through and the change of light made Dan squint. It reminded him of having to close his eyes when the flames in the crash reached his face. The nausea that caused departed as he became used to the light. They passed through a set of doors at the far end and left the building.

It was indeed a lovely day. Perfect, in fact. Not a breath of wind and just enough cloud to ensure it wasn't too warm. Tracy pushed her charge towards a group of four other patients in wheelchairs and a neat gap between them made her intentions clear.

'Don't put me there.'

'Sorry?'

'Don't put me with those people – I don't know them.' Dan spoke out of the corner of his mouth as they were approaching fast.

'Nonsense,' Tracy replied. 'Regular social contact is an important part of your recovery. It will improve your mood and make you less miserable.'

'But I like being miserab... Hello! My name's Squadron Leader Dan Stewart.' The four of them barely seemed to register his presence. *Typical*, Dan thought.

One of them spoke. 'Squadron leader? That's a bit pretentious, isn't it?'

Dan didn't even look at him. 'Tracy?'

'Yes, Dan?'

'I'm hallucinating again. I'd be grateful if you would take me back to my room, please.'

She put her hands on her hips. 'Make an effort!'

Dan thought he already had but tried again anyway – sort of. 'It would be pretentious if I were *not* a serving officer of that rank in Her Majesty's Royal Air Force, but if you mean am I a snob? Then yes I am – and proud of it.' He tried making himself look taller in the wheelchair, but it was more comfortable to settle back into it.

'I suppose you want me to call you "Sir".'

Tracy intervened. 'Boys! Be friends.'

Dan thought it was like being back at prep school only he was being forced to make friends with a kid from the state school next door. He looked at the oik

and realised they had something in common after all –
fire-damaged skin.

'You're not taking your medication, are you?' the
oik said to him. 'I can always tell – he's not taking
his either.' He gestured to the man next to him, who
seemed to be unaware of the temporary attention. 'He
is, though – not sure about her.' He pointed out the
remaining two in the group, who seemed to be just as
oblivious.

The oik appeared to know something so Dan made
an attempt to get it out of him. 'What's your name?'

'Gary. Although you'll probably insist on calling me
"Corporal", because I was in the army.'

'That won't be necessary.' Dan winced at how
arrogant that must have sounded.

'Very generous of you,' Gary predictably replied.

Dan tried again. 'What are you in for?'

Gary looked at him with disdain. 'You make this
place sound more like a prison than a hospital. Which it
may as well be – feels like I've been incarcerated in here
for years.'

His depressing manner reminded Dan of Eeyore
from *Winnie the Pooh*. The question was rephrased. 'I
mean, what's wrong with you?' Dan realised he wasn't
exactly ingratiating himself with Gary, but didn't care.

Gary cocked his head to one side and paused before
answering. 'You're definitely not taking the drugs.
Same as you, of course – have you looked at yourself
lately?'

Dan knew what he meant. All five of them shared

what seemed to be the now obligatory burns and accident damage to their hands and faces.

Tracy and another nurse arrived with trays of hot food and slotted them into place on the arms of the wheelchairs – all except for Dan's.

'Where's mine?' Dan could feel himself sounding more like a child all the time.

'Doctor Adams says you're to get it yourself – you need the exercise.'

'Charming! Just who does that stuck-up excuse of a human being think he is?' Dan turned to Gary for moral support, but the other man just smirked.

'Welcome to the club, comrade.'

Dan assumed Gary wasn't particularly fond of Doctor Adams either – that made two things they had in common.

Gary reached down to his bacon sandwich and lifted a corner of it. Tomato ketchup ran out like blood. The sight made Dan nauseous.

Gary stopped grinning. 'Ketchup,' he moaned. 'Never brown sauce – always red.'

Dan lost his appetite. 'I think I'll give it a miss, Tracy – thanks all the same.'

'Nonsense, you're coming with us.' She lifted away his blanket, put it over her shoulder, and held her hands out to him. 'Come on, let's try standing up.'

'You're joking, aren't you? I haven't stood up for, er, days? Weeks?'

'All the more reason to then.'

Dan knew it was pointless arguing and, anyway, he

had to start getting fit sometime. He reached out to take her hands and the other nurse moved to his side. Dan grasped, but stopped when pain wracked him. He tried letting go, but the two women had other ideas and, the next thing Dan knew, he was in a standing position. The pain dissipated.

'Now, that wasn't too bad, was it?'

Dan had to agree. The feeling was incredible. Like being set free. He looked down at Gary in more ways than one, before saying to Tracy: 'Come along, my dear, allow me to escort you.'

Gary said something sarcastic which Dan ignored. He tried walking normally, but all that happened was the bottom half of his body remained in situ while the top half tried to overtake it.

'Whoa!' said Tracy, catching him before he fell over. 'One step at a time.'

Dan recalled Adams saying the same thing. Dan couldn't even manage that. Elation turned to disappointment – Gary tittering through his sandwich didn't exactly help.

Tracy persisted. 'Come on. Try moving your right leg.'

Dan looked down. There was grass beneath his feet. Small wild flowers too. He suddenly got the feeling he was being played for a fool.

Dan didn't know why, but knew there was more to this than much-needed exercise. He looked up, expecting to see Doctor Adams and, sure enough, there he was – just a few yards away. A sensation of dread washed over Dan.

His right foot left the ground and Dan realised one of the nurses was taking the pace for him. Tracy had moved to his other side for support and, as she pulled him forward, he had no choice but to lift his left foot to join his right. Two more steps were taken like this, before Tracy decided he'd got the message. The next thing Dan knew, he was staggering like Frankenstein's monster towards his creator, with Tracy and the other nurse nearby – just in case.

After thirty seconds or so all three reached the doctor. Dan was shattered, but very pleased with himself. He was out of breath and had to take a deep lungful just to speak.

'Go on,' he gasped. 'Say "interesting".'

'Actually, I think "well done" would be more appropriate.' Adams paused before saying: 'Well done.'

Dan still couldn't warm to him. He assumed Gary couldn't warm to either of them. Adams looked down before he next spoke.

'Help yourself to some food, Dan.'

Dan followed the doctor's gaze and realised he was now standing next to a barbecue where sausages, burgers, steaks, chops, and various other meats were all sizzling and popping away. Fat was dripping onto the hot coals beneath, which caused tongues of fire to leap up and envelop them.

The distinct smell and look of the burning flesh caused Dan's nausea to return and he became dizzy. He put out his right hand to steady himself only to watch in helpless horror as it plunged towards the flames.

Adams and the nurses grabbed their patient just in time but, instead of steadying him, laid Dan down on his side. His head was so close to the grass he could see the individual blades and even the wild flowers nestling within. A bumble bee flew into view.

CHAPTER THREE

'When are you coming home, Daddy?'

Dan opened his eyes. He was back in his bed. Lucy was sitting next to it. He felt for the buzzer and pressed it. 'Er, soon darling, soon. Daddy's not been very well.'

'But it's been ages and I hate it when you're not there. It's not fair.'

She pulled the teddy bear she was holding closer to her. Dan had a momentary flashback to Alice's doll. The door opened and Mike walked in. Dan beckoned him over and motioned for him to bend down so he could whisper.

'Silly question, Mike, I know, but... my daughter *is* sitting in that chair, isn't she?'

Mike looked at Lucy, back at Dan, smiled and nodded. Dan relaxed. Mike raised his eyes to the ceiling as he left.

'Oh, darling, you've no idea how pleased Daddy is to see you.'

He stretched out his arms to hug her, but hesitated when he saw how monstrous they looked. Lucy jumped off the chair and hugged him anyway. Claire was right. His appearance didn't seem to bother her at all.

'Oh, Daddy, please come home. It's not the same without you. Mummy tries really hard, but she's not as good as you at reading stories and she doesn't play *any* games.'

Claire and Dan were used to Lucy playing them off against each other.

'Now, I'm sure that's not true, darling. And you have to understand that while Daddy's in hospital, Mummy has to work twice as hard and you must help her – by being twice as good. Okay?'

Lucy dropped her head and stuck out her bottom lip. Dan would normally push it back in with his finger before tickling her under the chin, but he didn't want his hands anywhere near her face.

'What's that noise?' Dan looked towards the door.

Lucy started giggling as if she knew what was coming.

'There it is again!' He looked out of the window. 'And again!' Dan glanced towards a wall and then back at his daughter. 'Can't you hear it?'

Lucy shook her head, still giggling. Dan farted.

'You must have heard it that time!'

Lucy broke into fits of laughter and ran out of the room, holding her nose.

Dan flopped back on the bed and stared up at the ceiling in his own fit of giggles. He calmed. 'Ah, kids, eh?' he said, to no one in particular.

'What about them?'

Dan continued to stare up at the ceiling. He was getting used to Adams appearing out of thin air. 'Only a man with no children of his own would say such a thing.' He turned to look at the doctor. He was holding a tray of food.

'As you missed lunch, it occurred to me you might still be hungry.'

Dan inclined the back of his bed, took the tray and lifted the lids. Bacon, sausage, steak, lamb chops, and – red sauce. He salivated. Ignoring any pain, Dan picked up some cutlery and dived in. 'Got to hand it to you, Doc,' he managed to get out between mouthfuls. 'Your "throw 'em in at the deep end" method certainly worked.'

'It's called exposure therapy,' Adams explained. 'Expose a patient to the very fear that's causing them problems and hope for the best.'

'Hufm fu the bess?'

'Well, it's not an exact science, but then that's mental illness for you. Particularly when it's made more complicated by other issues.'

Dan swallowed what he was eating. 'What other issues? Like the crash, you mean?'

'Something like that.'

Dan put down his knife and fork. 'You're like a policeman – never off duty. What are you up to now?'

Adams poured out a beaker of water and offered it. 'Still think I'm trying to kill you?'

Dan grasped the cup and drained the contents. 'No, but why do I get the feeling there's more to you than meets the eye?'

Adams leaned forward as if offering a chance to answer that. 'Paranoia, perhaps?'

Dan leaned away. The doctor stood back again and took out his notepad and pen.

'Mind if I ask you some questions?'

'If you must.'

'What's your name?'

'Seriously?'

The doctor just poised his pen. Dan sighed. 'Squadron Leader Daniel Stewart.'

'How old are you?'

'Thirty-six.'

'What year is it?'

'1966 – August the something.'

'Who's the prime minister?'

'Harold Wilson.'

'Who won the World Cup?'

Dan just looked at him.

'Oh, yes – I forgot.'

'Now there's irony for you,' Dan said, sarcastically.

The doctor ignored him. 'When did you break your arm?'

'Two weeks ago.'

'Describe what happened.'

Dan went through the events; from when he was standing by the hospital's barbecue, to passing out at the sight of the flames around the meat, to putting his hand into the hot coals, to slipping as he leapt back, to striking his head and breaking his arm as he fell, to lying on one side with his face in the grass, to looking at the wild flowers – and a bumble bee. Adams made some notes while Dan went back to eating and talking.

'How did you get the bumble bee to fly past me at exactly the right time?'

'I had it in a matchbox and released it as you fell.'

'That was a bit lucky, wasn't it? It could have gone anywhere.'

'Well, when you do it every day, luck becomes less of an issue.'

Dan stopped eating. 'You mean to say you've been staging that little stunt for me *every day* for the last two weeks?'

'More or less – only when the sun was shining, though. Bees have a habit of going to sleep when it's too cold.'

Dan didn't know whether to be impressed or scared.

Adams continued. 'Why do you think you passed out?'

'I guess the flames around the meat must have reminded me of what happened in the crash.' Dan glanced at his right hand and grimaced.

'Describe something you did yesterday.'

Dan swallowed his last mouthful and placed the knife and fork together on the empty plate. He shook his head.

'Describe something you did last week or last month.'

He shook his head again.

'Describe what happened in the aircraft crash.'

It dawned on Dan that everything he thought he knew about the crash was actually from the accident in the hospital. He shook his head yet again.

'Interesting.'

Adams' reply came as no surprise to Dan whatsoever. He was worried, though. 'What if I wake up tomorrow and I've forgotten the accident again – or even this conversation?'

The doctor appeared to give the question careful thought. 'That is a possibility, but today is the first time you've remembered what happened a fortnight ago, and certainly the first time you've eaten a hearty meal, so hopefully you'll retain it – we'll soon find out.'

Dan tried to get his head around the idea of waking up every day for the rest of his life forgetting the day before. Adams got up from his chair and approached the bed.

'You really ought to restart your medication, you know. You'll find it so much easier to remember what's been happening to you.'

Dan didn't think he needed to. 'If I can remember a relatively minor domestic accident without drugs, then I'll be able to remember the crash – it's only a matter of time.' One of the doctor's words struck him. 'Restart? You said *restart* my medication. Have I already been on it?'

Adams nodded.

'Then why did I stop taking it?'

The doctor produced a single red pill and placed it on the tray. 'Restart your medication and you'll find out.'

Dan picked up the tablet and squinted at it. 'I don't get you, Doc. You spend days trying to get me to remember one particular event, and yet you just stood back and watched when I couldn't breathe earlier.' He regarded the other man directly. 'Trust me, that's something I will *never* forget.'

Adams was unmoved. 'Take the pill, and you won't.'

Dan changed the subject. He looked past the doctor. 'Where's Lucy? Claire said she wouldn't be back until tomorrow, so how did she get here? Who's looking after her?'

There was a knock and a squadron colleague of Dan's put his head around the door. 'Tony!' Dan greeted him like a long-lost friend, but not before checking Adams could see him too.

'Am I interrupting?'

The doctor turned to Dan. 'I'll be in again first thing tomorrow morning as usual.' He gestured towards the pill. 'Let's hope I don't have to introduce myself again.'

Adams said something to Tony on the way out, which Dan couldn't hear. Tony nodded.

Seeing someone from his unit was a welcome relief for Dan. 'It's great to see you, Tony.' Tony put out a hand, but Dan moved his out of reach.

'Sorry, Tony. Hurts too much. Have you seen my daughter?'

Tony seemed to hesitate before answering. 'Yes, she's in one of the wards.' He appeared to pause again. 'Playing with a puppy.'

Dan was relieved, but puzzled. 'No wonder she hasn't come back – they allow animals in this hospital?'

'Therapy for the patients. Petting a dog or stroking a cat helps with anxiety, apparently.'

Dan disliked pets at the best of times, tending to view

them as consumers of cash at one end and producers of stuff you couldn't even put on the roses out of the other. And as for the hairs! He did feel guilty for not allowing Lucy to have a dog of her own, though – maybe Doctor Adams would let her play with a puppy in his room. That would work for both of them. His concerns returned.

'Did *you* bring Lucy here?' He noticed Tony hesitate yet again before replying.

'Yes, Claire asked me to. I collected her from school and brought her straight here.'

Dan became agitated. 'You collected her from school? How long have you been doing that?'

Tony picked up on the implication and tried to reassure his friend. 'Dan, I know things are tough for you right now, but it's been a struggle for Claire and Lucy too, so the squadron's rallying round to help – that's all.'

Dan calmed a little. Tony was right, of course. The military was excellent at looking after the families of service personnel and especially at times like this.

'Yes, of course. Sorry, Tony,' he acknowledged. 'I guess they're right – the crash has made me paranoid as well as forgetful.'

'Forgetful? That's putting it mildly. You can't remember a damn thing! Have you got that hundred quid you owe me?'

Dan smiled and began the questions he was desperate to have answers to.

'What do you know about the crash, Tony? Has the board produced a report yet? I can't even remember the investigation team visiting me for a statement, let alone the answers I gave.'

Tony didn't respond, which made Dan think he was encroaching onto an area they weren't at liberty to discuss. Maybe the flight *was* classified. 'I mean, we don't have to discuss the mission or the nature of the flight, or anything like that. Just the basics, like where it happened, was there anyone else involved, who got me out – that sort of thing. I can't even remember the type of aircraft I was flying, for goodness sake.'

Tony pulled up a chair and sat down. 'Dan, after your progress today, I hope it won't come as a surprise to learn you've been asking me those exact same questions every day since you stopped taking your medication.'

He indicated the red pill on the tray. Dan understood and nodded, before switching to a shake of the head. 'I don't want to take it.'

'Why not?'

'Because presumably it was my choice to stop… so why did I?'

'For goodness sake, Dan, you must have taken every pill and potion known to man over the last six months. What makes that one so special?'

'Exactly,' Dan replied, in some sort of 'Eureka!' moment. 'If they want me to take it, then why not give it to me normally? I mean, I must have to take other pills, so why not just put it in with those?' He picked up the tablet. 'Why has Doctor Adams singled out this particular one?'

Tony sighed. 'I have to get going – it gets pretty

boring talking to a guy who keeps repeating himself, you know.'

'Sorry, Tony. I guess I've been obsessing about this pill every day too?'

'Only since you stopped taking it – you were doing really well before that.' He turned to leave. 'Is there anything I can get you that you'll instantly forget having asked me for?'

Tony grinned and Dan took it as a challenge. He looked at the clock next to his bed. 'Yes, there is. I want a clock that works – not one of these stupid digital things – one with hands on it – right there.' He pointed to a spot on the wall at the foot of his bed.

Tony glanced at the 'digital thing'. 'Okay, this time tomorrow there'll be the biggest clock you have ever seen right in front of you and I bet you don't even notice it, let alone wonder where it came from.'

Dan shrugged in a 'see if I care' way, and looked out of the window to feign disinterest. His friend was about to walk out when Dan stopped him.

'Tony, what did Doctor Adams say to you just now?'

'Still feeling paranoid, eh?'

Dan was sheepish.

Tony smiled. 'He said: "Try and get him to take the pill."'

The door closed. Dan studied the pill once more and then the beaker of water.

'God, I thought he'd never leave.'

Dan reached for the buzzer.

'What is it about you military types? All this "stiff upper lip", "band of brothers" and thigh-slapping nonsense – it's enough to make you weep. Why can't you just face up to what's going on and accept it?'

The door opened. Dan didn't whisper this time.

'Sorry to bother you again, Mike, but is there someone sitting in that chair?'

Mike glanced at where Dan was pointing. 'Would you like a sedative?'

Dan looked at his hallucination.

Brian looked back. 'I'll only say what I have to say in your dreams – *or nightmares.*' He rubbed his hands together theatrically and deliberately cackled like a pantomime villain.

Dan refused the offer. Mike walked around the room to ensure Dan was alone. Brian stared at the male nurse as he did so.

'Just press the button again if you change your mind.' Mike took one last look at the empty chair and left.

'He's a queer. You can tell it a mile off – too well groomed for a real man, and he's a nurse for goodness' sake. What kind of guy chooses nursing for a career?'

Homophobia aside, Dan did think that strange but his hallucination concerned him more. 'What do you want, Brian?'

'Ah, now psychologically speaking, you're actually asking, what do *I* want. Being as I'm all in your head, figment of your imagination, repressed feelings, and all the other Freudian malarkey you care to mention. What do *you* want, Dan?'

'My hallucination to end, for a start.'

'Oh come on, don't be like that – make use of me. There's a good reason why what's left of your brain has conjured me up – it can't fix things conventionally, so is trying a hallucination instead. Desperate times and all that. Go on – ask me a question.'

Brian was looking smug, which always annoyed Dan. 'What caused the crash?'

Brian's shoulders dropped. 'Oh come on, if it was that easy, you'd have worked it out for yourself a long time ago. Your brain is damaged, Dan – whatever bridge or road led directly from that question to the answer has long since gone. What you need to do is find an alternative route.'

Dan groaned. 'I wouldn't know where to start.' He picked up the red pill. 'Why did I stop taking this?'

'Sorry, Dan – same problem. The link to the answer no longer exists. You've got to find a back road – while you still can.'

'What's that supposed to mean?'

Brian appeared to change the subject.

'Okay, how about I ask *you* a question? Or rather, I ask myself – or you – ask yourself a question if you know what I, er, you mean.'

Dan turned towards the window. It was getting dark. 'Brian, just do what you have to and leave or disappear or whatever.'

'Why do we dream? What's the purpose of it?'

Dan was beginning to tire, but decided to humour Brian. 'I don't know. To give the brain a rest or something?

I think I read somewhere it uses the time to reorganise itself for the following day, and it's during this process that we dream.'

'Exactly! The brain is basically an incredibly complex system of filing cabinets, and millions upon millions of times a day it pulls open a drawer, takes out a file, acts on whatever it says, puts it back in, and then closes the drawer again. But like most filing systems, a drawer sometimes gets stuck or won't open, or a file gets mislaid or put in the wrong drawer, and the brain uses sleep to sort all that out for the following day. It's the brain's accessing of those same files during sleep that conjures up the involuntary images and experiences we call dreams.'

Dan closed his eyes.

Brian persisted. 'Now, what do you think happens to all those filing cabinets when the brain gets damaged?'

Dan opened his eyes. 'They all fall on Brian and I can finally get some sleep?'

'No, they burst open and millions of files not only get lost or jumbled up, but so do all the individual pages, paragraphs, sentences, words – even the individual letters.'

Dan's eyes were getting heavy again. 'And I suppose you can no longer dream?'

'Maybe, but more importantly, your brain conjures up something to help you pick everything back up again – *me!*'

'And there was me thinking it was all bad news. I thought we were looking for roads?'

'We are, only they need building from scratch – letter by letter, word by word, sentence by sentence, paragraph, page, file, and finally, cabinet by cabinet – all the way to the answers.'

Dan closed his eyes again. 'Oh good. Wake me up when you've done that, will you?'

'Come on, Dan – take it seriously; let's make a start. Look at all the billions of jumbled-up letters in your head and pick one – any one.'

'Just go away, Brian.'

'How about this one: "P"?'

Dan sat up with a start. 'Passengers. There were passengers on the aircraft.'

'You didn't give me a chance to spell it out.'

'Shut up, Brian.' Dan focussed on the setting sun – the last rays of the day were about to disappear. 'I can't believe I missed it. It's been staring me in the face the whole time.'

'What has?'

Dan looked at his hands. 'All the injuries are at the exact same stage of recovery.'

'Well of course they are – you didn't burn your arms one day and your legs the next.'

Dan turned to Brian. 'You don't understand – every patient on this ward not only has similar injuries to me, but we're all at the exact same stage of recovery.'

'So?'

'Don't you get it? That means we were all injured *at the same time*. I crashed a *passenger* aircraft and the survivors are here with me to prove it.'

CHAPTER FOUR

'Good morning.'

He turned from the voice and groaned. 'What time is it?'

'Seven o'clock.'

Dan's fingers ached as he rubbed his eyes. He looked at the clock next to his bed and groaned again. 'Pointless looking at that thing. What are you doing in this early?'

Adams made another one of his intimidating lean-ins. 'I take it from that, you recognise who I am?'

The pillows stopped Dan from leaning away. 'Back off, Doc; it's too early for another one of your game—' He sat up, almost clouting the doctor with his forehead on the way. 'Yes… Yes… I do.' He thought for a second to ensure all the previous day's events were still there. They were – including his revelation about the other patients.

Dan smiled. 'Doctor Adams; Dan Stewart; thirty-six; 1966; Harold Wilson; England – next question!' The smile became a cheesy grin.

'Interesting.' The doctor was nothing if not consistent. 'Who won the World Cup?'

Dan grimaced. 'I don't know and I don't want to know. Where are those recordings you promised me?'

'*Very* interesting. On their way. Tell me first how you broke your arm.'

Dan went through the events as if it were a live commentary.

'Tell me about the aircraft crash.'

Dan shook his head. The doctor pulled up a chair, reached for his notepad and sat down.

'Tell me about your brother, Brian.'

'Doc, it's seven o'clock in the morning. Can't we do this after breakfast?'

An orderly walked in with a tray which told Dan he would once again be eating and answering questions at the same. He lifted the lids from the plates – cornflakes and a plate of bacon and eggs. The sight of two converging ova made him uneasy for some reason.

'I don't know; what do you want me to tell you?' Dan screwed up his nose as a prod of one of the eggs revealed it to be burnt with only the yolk salvageable.

'As you've probably noticed, Dan, we try to avoid asking leading questions for fear of putting ideas into the minds of patients who, out of either desperation or convenience, turn them into perceived memories. It's important all retrieved thoughts are genuinely your own.'

Dan cut away the burnt bit and placed it to one side. 'Well, just like all brothers, I suppose. Sometimes we get on. Sometimes we don't.' He cut off a piece of bacon and popped it into his mouth. 'More the latter than the former.'

'And why do you think that is?'

Dan pondered as he chewed. 'Well, although I'm

younger, I've achieved more professionally. Maybe he lives in my shadow.'

'Anything else?'

'We're just different. Different sense of humour, different standards, different friends, different dress sense – you name it.'

'And how would you feel if he suddenly died?'

Dan put down the knife and fork. 'Steady on, Doc. That's a bit heavy. Devastated, of course – he is flesh and blood after all.' He sniffed at the conjoined yolks before deciding to leave them.

Adams made his customary notes. 'Tell me about the hallucination you had last night.'

A piece of meat had become wedged between Dan's teeth. He probed it with his tongue. 'How do you know about that?'

'The duty log.'

Dan switched his attention to the bowl of cornflakes. 'It was Brian, of course.'

'How does Brian, your hallucination, compare to Brian, your brother?'

'Not a lot of difference really – just as vulgar, just as annoying.' He picked up a spoon. 'More helpful, I suppose.'

'In what way?'

'Well, I know his manifestation is just me trying to work things out in my own head, but I have to admit he is strangely cathartic.' Dan paused before qualifying: 'In an annoying way.'

'How did he help you last night?'

'It must have been something I already knew, but he

went rambling on about how the brain is a complicated filing system, which in my case had taken a knock, so all the cabinets and their contents are now strewn across the floor – right down to the individual letters apparently. He said he was there to help pick them all back up again. Nonsense, I know.'

Adams stopped writing and looked up. 'Well, it's certainly a bit simplistic to say the brain is an *orderly* filing system – probably more accurate to describe it as a *disorderly* filing system where individual letters are permanently strewn across the floor. For some reason, the brain is happy with this arrangement and to a certain extent can even cope if the disorder's caused by some kind of trauma. The real problem comes when the floor has holes in it and the letters become lost. We're pretty certain they can't be recovered.' He went back to his notes. 'So, you don't fear your hallucination?'

'Isn't that a leading question?' Dan said, smugly.

Adams didn't look up. 'I said we *try* to avoid asking leading questions – not forbid them.'

The doctor appeared to have an answer for everything.

'No, not at all.'

'So how would you feel if you never saw it again?'

Dan didn't answer straight away. 'Do you know, I think I would actually miss him? How strange is that?' He put his spoon into the cornflakes. 'Hey! They've forgotten the milk.'

'Did the hallucination of Brian help you to remember anything from the crash?'

'Hang on, Doc. I just need to ask for some milk.'

Dan pressed the buzzer. He then pretended to forget what had been asked.

'Sorry, what was the question?'

It was repeated but there was no way Dan was going to reveal what he'd worked out – not yet, anyway. He needed to question some of the patients first, and had a feeling Adams wouldn't like that.

'No, nothing I'm afraid. As I say, it was all just nonsense.'

The doctor closed his notepad and stood up. 'Do you have any questions for me?'

Dan thought for a second. 'I take it I can socialise with the other patients?'

Adams appeared cynical. 'I thought you didn't care for the company of strangers?'

'Well, I can't just stay in here all day – I'll go mad.'

They both looked at each other as if that particular Rubicon had already been crossed.

'Normal social intercourse is an important part of your recovery, so you not only can, but must.' Adams turned to leave. 'Just remember to be careful with what you say – no leading or personal questions. They'll only tell you exactly what you want to hear and vice versa.'

For a moment Dan thought the doctor was on to him. He did have a point, though.

Adams paused at the door. 'Have you decided to resume your medication?'

Dan didn't answer.

'Did you take the pill I left you?'

Dan turned to the window. 'Yes, I did. Maybe that's why I remembered who you were this morning.'

Adams walked back, put a hand into Dan's breast pocket and took out the red pill. 'Still suffering from paranoia or did amnesia make you forget?' He removed some fluff before replacing it. 'Of course, an attempt at deception could be a sign of psychological progress. Original thought needs some work, though.'

It was official. Dan couldn't stand the man.

Tracy passed him on his way out. She had her usual trolley, only this time there was a bowl with some towels and toiletries next to it. Dan became nervous.

'Good morning!' She was her usual bright and cheery self. 'Who's ready for a bed bath then?'

Dan gulped. She moved the trolley closer to his bed and removed the breakfast tray and stand. Dan forgot about the milk for his cornflakes and made a conscious effort to look out of the window.

'Looks like rain,' he said.

Tracy stopped what she was doing and looked out of the window too, moving into his line of sight as she did so. 'I think you might be right.'

Dan's nervousness disappeared. *That's strange*, he thought.

She faced him. 'Right, are we going to behave ourselves or am I going to have to get Mike to give you a bath instead?'

Dan recalled Brian's homophobic diatribe. 'No! I mean, that's okay. I'll be good.'

He thought he must have sounded like a small boy

again. Tracy smiled and began pulling the curtain around his bed to screen it off. The differences he was sensing became more pronounced. Dan didn't know whether it was the smell of the soap or the steam rising from the bowl, but he became relaxed – secure, even.

Tracy pulled the curtain across the window so he could no longer make use of it as a distraction. It didn't bother him. Dan found himself taking more of an interest in Tracy's preparations than in her. *Really strange*, he thought. He looked at her breasts as they did their usual dance, to prove something had changed in him. Nothing about Dan's person danced in response. *Now, that's just bizarre*, he thought again.

'Dan, behave yourself. Women always know where a man's eyes are looking.'

He put his hands up in defence. 'Honestly, Tracy, I don't think of you like that any more – believe me.'

She poured some soap into the bowl. 'Really? Some women might be offended by that.'

Dan blustered. 'Oh no! It's not like that. What I mean to say is, I still think you've a very attrac—'

She interrupted him. 'It's okay, Dan, you're no different to any other man. You soon get bored and want to move on.' She winked.

'Tracy, seriously. Something's changing in me.' He stared straight ahead. 'And I'm not sure if I like it or not.' He thought for a moment. 'Tracy?'

'Yes, my fickle admirer?'

'They don't, er, put anything in the food, do they?' Dan glanced across at the breakfast tray.

Tracy stopped what she was doing. 'What? Like bromide? Something to suppress your, ahem, natural instincts?'

'Yes. Something like that.'

She burst out laughing. 'Dan, that's the last thing they want to do in this place. God knows, there's little enough life here as it is.'

Dan tried to dismiss the ridiculousness of his suggestion as easily as Tracy but paranoia wouldn't let him. She started to undo the buttons on his pyjamas. He put a hand on top of hers.

'I don't think I'm ready to see all of myself yet.'

Tracy reverted to a more caring tone. 'That's okay,' she soothed. 'I'm going to cover you in towels anyway. Put your head back.'

Dan stared up at the ceiling while Tracy finished removing his pyjamas and did as promised. The bath commenced and he became cosseted in the softness of her contact and the occasional waft of feminine perfume. He closed his eyes and found himself wandering back to less stressful times. Dan couldn't remember, but imagined that this was how it must have been when he was a small boy – Tracy's cleaning of his body felt caring as well as cleansing. He opened his eyes to look at her and thought he could see his mother. She was smiling at him.

'Happy, darling?' he thought he heard her say. He nodded and smiled back.

Dan caught a glimpse of his chest. All the hair from it had burnt away and the way the remaining skin clung to his ribs reminded him of a rotting carcass. It should have turned his stomach, but he was in the care of his mother now, so everything was fine. Dan's transformation from Tracy's sexual predator to her compliant patient appeared to be complete.

'Do you want me to clean your penis or do you want to do it?'

Tracy's frankness interrupted the dream-like state. Dan gathered his thoughts to work out what that would entail, and decided the requirement for two hands made it impossible for him.

'You do it please, Tracy.' He put his head back again while his manhood received the fastest and least caring personal attention, ever. Dan winced throughout. 'Women really do hate men, don't they?' he found himself saying out loud.

'Best to get it over and done with in my experience,' Tracy replied, flatly. She reached for a clean pair of pyjamas and helped him to get into them. Her bubbly nature returned. 'What shall we do today, then?'

'Have I got you to myself?' Dan was pleased.

'Well, not constantly, but I'll be around until I go off shift.'

Dan was disappointed, but soon perked up at the thought of his mission. 'This may come as a surprise to you, Tracy, but I think I'd like to talk to some of the other patients today.'

Tracy ceased buttoning and looked at him. 'Are you feeling okay?'

'Never better.'

Tracy regarded the remains of the eggs on his breakfast tray. 'Well, if they are putting something in your food, I can only say I approve.' She picked up a toothbrush. 'Do you want to do it? I can put the toothpaste on for you if you like?'

Dan nodded.

'You can take your medication at the same time.'

Dan shook his head. Tracy reached into her pocket and pulled out a plastic tub with a couple of pale-looking tablets inside. Dan peered at them.

'What are they?' he asked suspiciously.

'Just antibiotics for your arm. Of course, if you don't want it to get better…'

Dan took the tub from her. Tracy poured him a beaker of water and he swallowed the tablets. They were probably safe to take, as unlike the red pill they hadn't been deliberately singled out. He tapped his left breast pocket before realising it must still be in his other pyjamas. It wasn't. Tracy was ahead of him and opened her palm to reveal it. Dan smirked before placing the pill into his new pocket and tapping it again. Tracy just shook her head.

Dan brushed his own teeth, and this small demonstration of independence boosted his morale enough to make his own way to the wheelchair this time. Tracy pushed him out into the corridor, where the door opposite was open. He was surprised to see the room empty.

'What happened to the chap in there?'

Tracy hesitated before answering. 'He's gone home – lucky thing.'

'But he came in with me.'

'What makes you think that?'

Dan paused this time. 'Er, well, he had the same injuries as me.'

Tracy seemed puzzled. 'Just because a patient appears to present with the same symptoms doesn't mean their treatment and recovery will be the same.'

Yeah, right, Dan scoffed to himself. They made their way down the corridor as before. 'Where are we going?'

'If it's going to rain today, everyone will be in the conservatory. You'll be able to make lots of new friends there.' Dan enjoyed the maternal side to Tracy, but didn't have much time for the patronising one.

They entered the conservatory, where some of the patients were sitting, either reading, writing, or in quiet contemplation. A quick scan confirmed they all had facial injuries of one sort or another – Dan's passenger conviction was off to a good start. He motioned Tracy to park his chair opposite Gary who grimaced as if a bad smell had just been placed in front of him.

Dan attempted to start the conversation with an uncharacteristic bit of cheer. 'Good morning, Gary!'

'Morning, Brigadier.'

Dan bit his lip to stop himself from rising to the bait. Silence followed, during which Tracy switched her attention back and forth between them.

'Well, as you two boys seem to be hitting it off, I'll leave you to it.' She turned on her heels and did just that.

Dan tried again. 'Lovely day!'

A sporadic tap made Gary look up towards the roof

of the conservatory. The raindrops became a continuous drum.

'Well, I suppose if I were on fire I would find it welcoming.'

Dan dropped the social pretence the moment he heard the word 'fire'. 'What do you remember about the crash?' He frowned and imagined his ear being tweaked by Doctor Adams. 'No leading questions!' he could hear him say.

'Crash?' Gary asked.

'Forget that, er, well, don't forget it, but… um.' He'd only just started and was already making a hash of it. Dan's determination to get to the truth was hindering him. He repeated the next question in his head a few times to make sure it sounded right. 'Tell me how you came by your injuries.'

Gary glanced left and right, as if to make sure nobody else was listening. He leaned forward and beckoned Dan to do the same, which he eagerly did.

'Mind – your – own – business.' Gary sat back and picked up a crossword book.

Dan threw the doctor's rulebook out of the window. 'Look, Gary. We both know why we're in here. I just want to know what you know about it – that's all.'

Gary didn't take his eyes away from the puzzle. 'I don't talk to anybody in this place who doesn't take their prescribed medication. It's a waste of time. You may as well talk to a madman.' He looked up. 'Any offence taken, gladly given.' He looked back down again before continuing. 'Everybody here suffers from one or more serious psychological illnesses, so to refuse help with that is, ironically, mad.'

Dan stayed silent for a few seconds. 'You practised that little speech, didn't you?'

Gary put the crossword down and leaned forward again. 'Take the pill, Dan, and we'll talk again.'

Dan smiled. 'You called me Dan.'

Gary didn't respond. Dan wondered who to approach next when he made eye contact with a woman who waved excitedly for him to join her. He reverted back to type and stuck his nose in the air.

'It would appear someone wants to talk to me.'

Gary ignored that too.

Tracy was nowhere to be seen, so Dan decided to make his own way over. He went to release the brakes on the wheelchair, but thought walking the six paces would do him some good. Her sex was the real reason, of course – Dan didn't want her thinking he needed a wheelchair. The fact that every step made him look like a drunk at kicking-out time didn't seem to worry him, for some reason, although when he saw the burns to her face close up, Dan did wonder why he'd bothered. His conscience ensured he felt guilty at this shallowness.

'Did I hear you two talking about the crash?'

Dan became interested in her again. 'Yes! What do you know about it?' He congratulated himself on asking a question Adams would have been proud of.

'Well, it was terrible. Bodies everywhere.'

Dan winced at the frankness, but no matter how upsetting, he had to know what happened.

'People screaming, calling for loved ones, sirens, blue flashing lights – just terrible.'

He interrupted her. 'Where did we crash?' Dan reasoned it was safe to start asking leading questions.

She stared into the distance.

The lady seemed to be drawing knowledge from something that was out there. Dan envied her that.

'London, I think.'

Dan slumped back in the chair. He had believed there might be the chance of ground casualties, but crashing an aircraft into the middle of a city made that all but inevitable. The death toll could have run into thousands. He put his head into his hands as he tried to comprehend that. Guilt was becoming his main emotion. Maybe that was the reason why he'd stopped taking the drug – he felt responsible for everyone's suffering and wanted to end it all? He felt for the pill to make sure it was still there.

'Look – there's another ambulance.'

She was still staring into the distance and Dan followed her gaze – to a television set. It appeared to be tuned to a hospital-themed drama.

Tracy appeared. 'Shall I turn the volume up on the telly a bit?'

Dan shook his head. He looked around the room. Other than Gary, every single person was either asleep, talking to themselves, or otherwise engaged in an activity that made it clear they weren't themselves – they all appeared mentally ill in some way. Surely not every crash survivor had a brain injury as well as breaks and burns? Dan's morale slumped as he realised he might have to look elsewhere if he was to get to the bottom of the crash.

'Just take me back to my room please, Tracy.'

She brought the wheelchair over and helped him into it. They were about to leave when Dan spotted Alice at the exit. He asked Tracy to stop by her. Seeing Alice again, he realised there must have been at least some ground casualties, as military aircraft rarely allowed families on board. The thought that he could be responsible for her mother's death made him desperate to make amends in some way.

She was again wearing the all-encompassing cerise dressing gown with the doll still as close as she could get it. Her head was down as before, but this time Dan could just make out the tip of a nose and the slit of a mouth – both horribly burnt. As usual, he was lost for words, but felt it only right to show his compassion by putting a hand on hers. The grotesque appearance of both meant he had to force himself to do it. She placed her other hand, or rather what was left of it, on top of his, making him uneasy.

'Mummy came back today. She wants to thank you.'

Dread descended on Dan. Alice pulled his hand closer to her and he had to make a conscious effort not to snatch it away. She looked up at him and smiled.

'Thank you for caring, Dan.'

The smile distorted what remained of her features –

like a living corpse from a horror movie. Dan knew who the real monster was. She dropped her head again and to Dan's relief, let go. Tracy assumed the conversation was now over and wheeled him back into the corridor.

'Well, I think you have a secret admirer there. I might be jealous!'

'Don't joke about such a thing, Tracy. It doesn't become you.' They continued in silence.

Although Dan felt deflated over his lack of success with the survivors, he was content for the consistency of their injuries to confirm his discovery, especially as Gary was prepared to talk about the crash. Once Dan had resumed his medication, of course. *That damn pill*, he thought. *Messing with my and everybody else's minds.* He pondered that before raising the back of his hand.

Tracy stopped. 'Yes, your Lordship?'

'I'm not in an ordinary ward, am I?'

She turned to face him. 'What makes you say that?'

Dan presented his evidence. 'I have a brain injury and Alice clearly has a similar issue. The lady I spoke to thought a drama on the television was real and Gary said: "*Everybody* here suffers from one or more serious psychological illnesses."' He looked up at her. 'Is this a neurological ward?'

Tracy raised her eyebrows, as if impressed by his sleuth-like deduction. She went back to pushing him. 'Not just a ward; the whole hospital specialises in neurology.'

They reached the door to his room, to be greeted by smiles from Claire and Tony walking towards them. Claire was ahead, and the first thing Dan noticed was

Tony dropping his hand from the small of her back. He tried not to read anything into it.

'Wonderful to see you up and about, Dan.' Claire leaned forward and kissed him on the cheek. She seemed to ignore his lips.

She used to call me 'darling' too, he thought.

'We'll take it from here thanks, Tracy.'

Tony took Tracy's place, while she held the door open for them all to enter. Claire went straight into mother mode.

'Look what we've brought for you!' she enthused.

The contents of a carrier bag were emptied onto the bed. There were chocolates, sweets, fruit, socks, underwear, and all the other paraphernalia needed for long-term involuntary incarceration. Some items remained in the bag, which Claire asked Tony to deal with for some reason. He reached in and pulled out a large analogue clock. They both regarded Dan with enthusiasm.

'You lied to me.' The tone of Dan's voice made them drop their smiles. 'You said it would be the *biggest* clock I had ever seen.'

Tony laughed and Claire burst into tears of relief.

'You remembered! That's fantastic news!'

Both Tony and Claire embraced him.

'Steady on, you two. I am ill, you know.' Dan had parked his misgivings about them.

'You don't understand,' Claire said. 'That's the first time I've seen you remember *anything* new in months!'

In that context, Dan appreciated his progress must

seem like a miracle, so he put up with the aches and pains her hugs were causing him.

'And that's not all!' Tony said.

He picked up a remote control and a screen in the corner of the room burst into life with the unmistakable footage of two football teams being led out onto a pitch.

Dan recalled the match like it was yesterday. 'The World Cup final. England beat West Germany four–two after extra time – Geoff Hurst scored a hat-trick.'

Claire and Tony burst into yet more cheers and tears, before jumping up and down and hugging each other this time.

'This calls for a celebration!' Tony reached into the bag again and retrieved the last few items – a bottle of champagne and three glasses. 'I've been hanging on to these ever since you were first admitted.'

He popped the cork and began pouring. Claire passed Dan the first glass. The sight of his injured hand being magnified by the liquid through the glass refocussed the elephant in the room of full recovery. He was about to take a sip when the door opened.

'No alcohol, I'm afraid.'

'Come on, Doc,' Tony interjected. 'Surely he's allowed one sip?'

'One drop of alcohol is enough to put back months of progress. I'm sorry.'

Adams was right of course, but he sure knew how to kill a moment. Dan wondered what or who else he might have killed – or bored to death.

'But he remembers things.' It was Claire's turn to try and speed up her husband's return to normality.

'Sorry, nothing we're not expecting. I'm afraid we must allow the treatment to continue.' He turned to his patient. 'Assuming Dan's now ready to restart it?'

Dan passed a suspicious eye over the three of them. 'I want to get a few things straight first.'

All three looked back at him with keen anticipation.

'I *think* I crashed an aircraft six months ago. Did that actually happen?'

They nodded in unison.

'I *think* there were passengers on my aircraft. Was that true?'

All three nodded again.

'I *think* at least some of those passengers are here with me on this ward. Is *that* true?'

And again.

'Hmmm. I *think* fairies live at the bottom of my garden.'

Claire and Tony responded positively, but Adams didn't.

Dan became agitated. 'This is just nonsense. What sort of "treatment" involves your wife and closest friend deliberately lying to you? I expect to receive the odd white lie from doctors, but family? Why are you doing this?' Claire and Tony hung their heads.

Adams interjected.

'It's not their fault, Dan. Your treatment requires your memories to be recovered by your own initiative, with uncontrolled accidental or deliberate attempts to influence your thinking avoided wherever possible.

That's why the questions I ask you are nearly always open-ended. Understand?'

'Well, what about the stunt you pulled at the barbecue?'

'That was designed to recover a particular memory. If I thought putting you in a burning aircraft wouldn't kill you, I would do the same at the crash site.'

Dan didn't know what to think. Up until now he'd felt he was making steady progress, but with nothing to confirm whether his thoughts were real or imaginary, how could he be sure? How could he be sure of anything? Names? Dates? Times? When he was dreaming? When he was awake? Was he eating when he thought he was? Was he thinking now or talking aloud? And what about his emotions? Did he dislike Tracy, but like Doctor Adams? Do they even exist? Does any of this exist? Maybe everything was a hallucination, like Brian.

Dan took a deep breath. 'I know my hallucination of Brian is not real. So, I'm going to assume that because I've never thought the same of you or anybody else, then this hospital must actually exist and my situation must, therefore, be real.'

Claire and Tony appealed to the doctor who knelt down to Dan's level.

'Dan, you have made more progress in the past twenty-four hours than in the whole of the last six months. Your brain is finally coming to terms with reality but under constant stress.' He pointed to Dan's pocket. 'The red pill will fix that.'

Dan remained silent while trying to make sense of it all. He eventually spoke. 'You've all admitted lying to me. I need time to think about that – please leave.' He glared at Claire and Tony. 'All of you.'

Claire started to cry. Tony put his arm around her and Adams motioned for them all to go. Claire turned back to Dan as they walked out of the door.

'Everything we've done, and are doing, is for you, Dan. Please understand that.' She was still sobbing as they left.

'Well, that could have gone better.'

'Fuck off, Brian.'

'And I thought I was supposed to be the vulgar one.'

'I said: fuck off.'

'Okay, okay, but you might want to take a look out of the window before they leave.'

Dan looked up to find Brian gone.

He made his way to the window, holding on to the sink for support. From his bed, he could only see the sky and tops of trees, but he now had a view of the ground below and the visitor car park opposite. He soon saw the familiar shapes of Claire and Tony making their way towards it.

His wife was leaning on Tony for support and, even though Dan hated it, she needed that right now. He made a decision. Whatever the rights or wrongs of the situation, he had to get better for her – for her and Lucy, and right now.

Dan placed a beaker under the cold tap and half-filled

it with water. He watched as Tony and Claire stopped at the entrance to the car park and turn to face each other. Dan took the red pill out of his pocket and placed it on his tongue. He raised the cup to his lips just as Tony raised Claire's lips to his.

CHAPTER FIVE

'I'm really sorry, Dan.'

'What's it all about, Brian?' Dan continued to stare out of the window even though Claire and Tony had long since departed. 'What's the point of being born, growing up, having a life, getting married and starting a family, just for one single event to end it all?'

Brian looked at him.

'I mean, I could understand if it took another thirty-six years to destroy what's taken thirty-six years to create, but how does just one moment of madness end *everything*?'

Brian appeared not to know what to say.

Dan turned to him. 'Do you want to know what I think?'

Brian still said nothing.

'I'll tell you what I think – no, I'll tell you what I *know* and that is: *there is no God*. And do you want to know how I know there is no God?'

Brian carried on looking at Dan in silence.

'Because, if having a life and a family is *good* and being nearly burnt to death in an aircraft crash is *bad*, then logic would seem to dictate evil is more powerful than good, for what it took God thirty-six years to create, the Devil destroyed in less than thirty-six minutes.' Dan went back to staring out of the window. 'Now, as God is meant to be more powerful than the Devil when he's clearly not, one has to assume the Devil is our true lord and master, or…' He looked at the pill in the cup – it was turning the water red. 'It's all a crock of shit.'

Dan glanced at his reflection in the mirror above the sink before hurling the cup at it. He set about throwing anything he could lay his hands on.

Brian broke his silence. 'Now come on, Dan.' He ducked to avoid a bar of soap, even though there was no need. 'You've got to focus on what you still have.'

Dan picked up a bar of chocolate and threw it against a wall. It rebounded limply. 'You mean, what I'm still going to lose!' He searched for something heavier.

'Think about Lucy.'

Dan spotted the oranges Claire had brought. 'And what do you know about kids? You've never even been married.' The fruit was hurled in different directions.

'Okay, so I don't have kids of my own, but I'm still her uncle and I don't want her to lose you.'

'Lose me? She lost me the second I was incinerated. What six-year-old wants a walking corpse for a father?' The oranges resulted in yet more unsatisfactory thuds.

'She doesn't care what you've become or look like – you know that. She just wants her daddy back.'

Dan picked up Tony's clock. 'Well, it looks like Tony's replaced me in the bedroom, so why not go the whole hog and replace me as a father, too?'

He threw the clock as hard as he could. It bounced off the window, but not before leaving a small crack. Dan picked up the champagne bottle.

'God, Dan! NO!'

'I've already told you, *God doesn't exist*.'

Brian tried to block the projectile, but it passed through him just as easily as it did the window. The sight of glass shattering produced a grin on Dan's face. The sound of a bottle exploding on the pavement below followed by a squeal of brakes just sealed the sense of satisfaction. Dan flopped onto the bed, exhausted.

'Now, that's what you call a champagne celebration!'

The door burst open and two orderlies rushed in, followed by Doctor Adams. They pinned Dan to the bed, rolled up a sleeve and the contents of a syringe was emptied into his arm. Given his weakened state, Dan thought their reaction a little over the top but then felt obliged to add his own performance to the theatrics. He looked at Adams while presenting his best *Julius Caesar*.

'Et tu, Brute?' Dan started giggling and passed out.

He had a dream. He was standing in a snow-covered landscape with nothing to be seen in all directions. The snow was moving and taking him with it. Dan took a step back, but the snow continued to move him forward in the same direction. A black dot appeared in the distance. Before long, people appeared too. Dan had a feeling he knew them, but they were too far away to identify.

Both they and he were all converging on the first

black dot, which seemed to be growing in size. Dan was on the cusp of identifying one of them when they reached the dot and disappeared. The dot was a hole in the ground, through which the snow and bodies were vanishing. More people Dan felt he should be able to recognise reached the hole and fell in too.

Dan paniced. He threw himself onto the ground in a desperate attempt to escape, but it was hopeless. The speed of the snow's movement increased as Dan approached the edge of the hole, and he thrust his arms and legs out in all directions, trying to get purchase.

Someone grabbed his hand – It was Lucy but she wasn't there to save him, as she too was being dragged towards the hole. They held on to each other as they passed over the edge, with Dan's free hand still clawing at the snow. At the very last moment, he found the rim and they stopped falling. Dan looked down at her.

The snow continued to pour like a waterfall over and around them, but Dan managed to keep a firm grip of his daughter's hand. He could see movement lower down and realised she was holding Claire's hand, which in turn was holding on to Tony's. He couldn't see who Tony was hanging on to, but Dan was sure he knew them too, along with the many others underneath. They were all hanging there, waiting for Dan to save them.

Dan dug his nails into the rim in an attempt to pull them all out, but it crumbled, and each time he regained his grip, it crumbled some more. Dan saw Brian above and, when he realised his brother wasn't being dragged in too, screamed at him to help. To Dan's astonishment, Brian's response was to put a hand up as if he didn't want to be disturbed – he was staring into the fast-moving current, as if looking for something.

Dan had snow pouring into his eyes, ears and throat, and spat some of it out onto his outstretched arm. The spittle broke the snow out into individual flakes, but instead of being made up of crystals – they were letters. The snow was millions upon millions of tiny white letters of the alphabet. Dan looked back up to see Brian put a hand into the torrent and take something out. Pleased with what he found, Brian then turned to Dan and presented him with a letter: 'T'.

'Cup of tea, dear?'

Dan woke with a start. Bright light made him screw his face up and he raised a hand to try and squeeze out a sudden migraine. He turned in the direction of the voice. His vision and head cleared at the same time to see a tea lady with her trolley.

'Milk and sugar?'

She stirred the tea and placed it next to his bed – his new bed. Dan glanced in the direction of the window to see it was now a wall. He then looked to where the broken digital clock would have been – it was no longer there. *The things I have to do to get rid of that stupid clock*, he said to himself. Dan was about to survey the rest of the room when he came face to face with Tracy. She had her hands on her hips and was tapping a foot – never a good sign in a woman.

'So, any free tickets to your next gig?'

Dan looked at her, confused. 'Gig?'

Tracy kept her hands in place. 'Well, we all thought after that little antic, it's clear you must be some spoilt brat of a rock star. What next? A television through the window, or are you going to drive your Rolls-Royce into a swimming pool?'

Dan shrank in her presence, but was determined not to be the little boy again. 'Tracy, my wife is having an affair.'

She launched at him. 'I don't give a damn if she's banging the entire England football team – you could have killed someone! You do something like that again and I will personally throw you out of the window afterwards.'

Given his weight loss, Dan was sure she was capable of that, but knew she just wanted to make a point. At least, he hoped so.

'Have I made myself clear?'

Dan sheepishly nodded.

'Right. Thanks to your childishness, we've lost a room, so you're going to have to double up with another patient for the time being.'

Dan now saw the second bed opposite him and fretted. 'Which one?'

'What?' Tracy still had her hands on her hips.

'Which patient? What if we don't get on?'

He knew he'd end up regretting throwing the champagne bottle out of the window sooner or later, but had hoped the feeling of euphoria would last just a little longer.

'You'll soon find out. Doctor Adams will be in shortly to see if there are any adverse effects to the sedative he had to administer, and then the physio will be in after that. Any questions?'

Dan shook his head.

Tracy marched to the door and opened it. 'Drink your tea before it gets cold.'

She nodded towards the mug and left. Dan picked it up and took a sip. He recalled Gary's comment about the hospital being like a prison and Dan worried who his cellmate would be. *Anybody but him*, he thought.

He pondered the dream. Brian and the letter aside, it was the people that intrigued Dan most; or, rather, the ones he recognised and, in particular, the order in which he saw them. It couldn't be more obvious. Lucy and he needed each other; but in turn, she needed her mother, who needed her and Tony, who needed her and whomever else he was hanging on to, and so on and so forth.

'So much for Brian's theory of no longer being able to dream,' he scoffed.

The door opened and in walked Adams with a woman Dan assumed to be the physiotherapist. Adams went straight into his usual series of questions, always culminating in the ones about the World Cup and the crash, both of which Dan still couldn't answer. It was beginning to annoy Dan that he'd yet to see any recordings of the matches despite being promised them.

There was another fruitless attempt at getting him to restart taking the red pill too, but those days were over.

No, there was only one thing Dan was interested in now, and that was getting physically fit enough to be a proper father to his daughter again. Cue the physiotherapist.

The doctor left and Dan made the introductions. 'Dan Stewart. Pleased to meet you. I thought we'd start with a few warm-up exercises in the gym, followed by some circuit training and then a run. Nothing too ambitious – say, a mile or so. What do you think?'

The physio reached across and took his left hand. Dan winced in anticipation, but there was no need to.

'Hello, Dan. My name's Lisa.'

Dan begrudgingly acknowledged her politer approach.

'Have you ever heard of the phrase "you have to learn to walk before you can run"?'

'Of course I have,'

Lisa smiled at him. 'Then let's start with a few baby steps – squeeze my hand as hard as you can.'

'But I'll hurt you.'

'Let me worry about that. Come on, squeeze my hand.'

Dan shrugged and pressed his fingers against hers.

Lisa stopped smiling. 'I said, squeeze it – hard!'

Dan sighed. 'Okay, if that's what you want.'

Ignoring his own pain, he gripped her hand with a pressure just short of what he thought would hurt – he was a gentleman after all. Lisa began smiling again. Dan gripped a little harder in response. She kept on smiling. Just about coping with what was becoming agony, Dan gripped harder still, but her expression didn't change.

Ignoring all accepted social boundaries between the sexes, Dan squeezed her hand as hard as he could. Lisa was still smiling.

Dan forgot to breathe, turned a bright shade of red, and collapsed in a drama of sweaty puffing and panting. He opened an eye mid-recovery in the hope of seeing Lisa just as stressed, but she was still standing there – smiling. Dan closed the eye and tried not to add her to a list that was starting to look a lot like an inventory of the entire human race.

Lisa let go and waited for Dan to recover.

'Okay?'

'Looks like I have a lot of work to do,' he admitted.

She examined his other hand. 'Well, there's strength in there somewhere. No one throws a magnum of champagne through a window without having at least some potential.'

Dan perked up. 'So, my fame's spreading, eh?' He particularly liked the exaggeration of the bottle's size. *That's how these things start*, he thought to himself. *It will be a jeroboam next week and a methuselah after that.*

Lisa raised her eyebrows. 'You were famous before that.'

Dan's mood dropped again as he recalled the incident with Tracy. He wondered if his weekly exaggeration theory also applied to penis size. It probably did – but in the opposite sense.

'Let's sit you up.' A click of the remote and a few seconds later Lisa had him in a semi-reclining position. 'Can you sit upright?'

Dan pulled his back up off the pillows the last few degrees, until it was at right angles to his legs. So far, so good.

'Stretch your arms out in front of you and spread your fingers – palms down.'

Dan did as he was told. Still good.

'Now turn your palms up.'

Again, no problem – even with the break to his forearm.

'Now make two fists.'

'Do I have to?'

Lisa regarded him as if it were a rhetorical question. Dan prepared himself for pain and began rotating the joints. It felt as if each were welded in position and he had to break them free again. Biting his bottom lip, Dan tried to ignore the sensation of bone grating against bone as they curled. He got about halfway when agony forced him to open them again.

'I guess there's some real damage there,' he said despondently.

Lisa massaged his fingers. 'Better?'

Dan nodded. Maybe he could grow to like her after all.

'Right. Let's take a look at the rest of you.'

Before Dan had a chance to protest, Lisa had undone the buttons of his pyjama jacket and whipped it off him. He closed his eyes, tight.

'Are you all right?'

'It's okay, Lisa. Just resting my eyes.'

'Well, while you've got them closed, point a finger with your left hand and touch your nose with it.'

He did as he was told and hit the bullseye. He opened his eyes and grinned. 'Not bad, eh?'

Dan found himself looking at his naked torso for the first time. Oddly, the sight didn't make him ill and he found that strange. He looked across his chest, stomach, and down both arms. None of it bothered him in the slightest, even though it was all horribly burnt, damaged, and wasted. 'Fascinating,' he thought he was saying to himself.

'What is?'

Lisa moved to his shoulders and felt her way across them.

'I don't know.'

Dan examined his chest more closely. It was only that morning he'd compared it to an animal's carcass but now it seemed to be more fleshed out – healthier. Pumped up, even. His ribs were still more visible than he would have liked, but it was almost as if the meat he'd had for dinner the previous night had gone straight to them. He studied his left bicep and moved his right hand across to touch it. It was still thinner than before the crash and the skin wrinkled easily, but it didn't seem to be as visually repulsive as he thought it would be. Dan looked more closely. The muscle underneath appeared to be—

'OW!'

Lisa had dug one of her knuckles into his shoulder. 'Does that hurt?'

He gave her a look but she carried on, regardless. Dan went back to examining his body. Preparing for the worst, he pulled back his left trouser leg, just as he had the day before, but even though his knee was still wider than his calf, it didn't seem to be as bad as he remembered.

'How strange.' He uncovered his right leg. 'Lisa?'

'Hmmm?'

'Do I look normal to you?'

She stood back. 'Pretty normal for a guy who's spent most of the last six months lying in bed doing nothing. Why do you ask?'

'It's just that yesterday morning, I couldn't stand the sight of my body but now...' He raised his right hand and looked at the back of it. 'It seems almost... natural.'

'Lie back.' Lisa took hold of the remote and his bed became flat again. 'I don't know. Acceptance of your situation perhaps? You'd need to speak to Doctor Adams on that one.'

Dan harrumphed. 'He just lies to me and encourages everyone else to do the same.' He narrowed his gaze at Lisa. 'Does that include you?'

Lisa thinned her lips in return. 'You know what they say when everyone else appears to be mad except you?'

Dan had been waiting for someone to say that. 'That the conspiracy theorists were right all along?'

She moved to his legs and rotated the joints. Dan gritted his teeth against the occasional ache and stab.

'So, you think this hospital is part of some conspiracy theory?'

'Well, something's not right.'

'Listen, the only conspiracy in this place is the one

that stops me getting a pay rise. Come on, let's try standing up.'

She put her hands out to him but Dan let her know he was capable of getting off the bed on his own.

'Take your hand off the bed rail.'

He did as asked, but then grabbed her still-outstretched hands instead. 'Shall we dance?'

'I don't know about dancing, but I've heard your walking's not too bad – come with me.'

She stepped backwards and Dan went with her. His neck ached so he tilted his head forward and found himself looking at her name badge. He looked back up.

'Lisa, how tall are you?'

'Five-eight. Maybe five-nine in these shoes.'

'But I'm nearly six feet and I'm looking up at you.'

She tilted her head to one side. 'Men – always exaggerating the size of something.'

'Seriously, Lisa. I'm a lot shorter than I used to be.'

'Well, your posture's not exactly helping – stand up straight.'

He did as told and it helped a little, but not the four inches or so he needed to regain. What struck Dan more than anything was that he should have been devastated by the height loss but wasn't. Almost as if he had always been that tall.

Lisa soon had him walking around like a toddler, which was progress, so Dan was pleased. She was right, of course. He was going to have to learn to walk all over again before he could even think about running. She finished up with a demonstration of the exercises he had to complete before her next visit, and left him with some literature and a sponge ball for hand exercises. Dan expected another lecture before she left about restarting his medication, but it didn't happen. He respected her for that.

He reached for his pyjama jacket to get dressed again when he saw Brian lying on the other bed. Dan spoke first for a change.

'Go on then. Say something disparaging about Lisa.'

'I don't know what you mean.'

'You're the most judgemental person I know. There's bound to be something about her you can't resist telling the world.'

'She seems like a nice person.'

'Is that it? Nothing about her being too skinny or having a flat chest that makes her a lesbian in your book?'

Brian got off the bed. 'You're the one saying it, Dan. Maybe the book belongs to you?'

Dan changed the subject. 'Anyway, you told me a brain injury means no more dreams, but I had the most vivid dream possible earlier.'

'Yes, I know. Good, wasn't it?'

'What do you know about it?'

Brian walked over and mimicked rapping Dan on the head with his knuckles. 'Dan, wake up. I'm in your head, remember? I not only know about it but produced, directed, and starred in it too! Well, co-starred.'

Dan sat on the edge of the bed and placed the jacket on his lap. '*You* made it happen?'

'Of course. Well, we both did, but I told you I was

here to help. What did you think of the snow actually being letters? Clever, eh?'

Dan recalled the sequence of events. 'You clearly weren't in it to help – why did you let us fall into the hole?'

Brian became confused. 'Us?'

'Yes, Lucy, Claire, Tony, me, and all the others.'

Brian returned to the other bed and sat down. 'They were in the dream too? I didn't see any of them – only you.' He appeared to ponder the significance. 'Interesting,' he finally said.

That's all I need, Dan thought, *my hallucination turning into my doctor.*

Brian stood up again. 'I deliberately let you fall into the hole because I wanted you to understand how serious things are. What did you do after you crossed over the edge and went into it?'

Dan searched his pyjama top. 'I made sure I still had hold of Lucy.'

'Before that. What stopped you from falling?'

Dan found a sleeve, put a hand in and pulled it up to his shoulder. 'Grabbing the edge, of course.'

'Then what happened?'

'Er, we stopped falling – remember?'

Brian approached him. 'What did you try to do then?'

'Pull us all out, of course.'

'And why couldn't you?'

'Because I was trying to pull everyone else up too?'

'No, the weight of all those people was academic – there was another reason you couldn't pull them out. Think.'

Dan reached around his back and flailed for the right sleeve. He stopped. 'The edge of the hole kept crumbling away.'

Brian remained silent.

'Anyway, it was the doc who first mentioned holes – not you.' Dan went back to finding the sleeve.

Brian leaned towards him. 'What happens to holes when their edges start to crumble?'

Dan let the jacket hang from his shoulder. It had dropped to his wrist when he realised where Brian was going with the conversation. 'They get bigger.' Dan grabbed the sleeve and pulled it back up again. 'Anyway, that's clearly not happening to me. My memory's getting better all the time.'

Brian looked him in the eye. 'Is it? Are you sure? How do you know you don't forget something again the second you've remembered it?'

'Well, mister smarty pants, Doctor Adams asks the same questions every time he sees me, and every time I give him the same answers – what I know I tell him, and what I don't – I don't.'

Brian stood back and folded his arms. 'Okay – what's your name?'

Dan let go of the sleeve again. 'Give it a rest, Brian. It's bad enough the doc sounding like a broken record.'

'I'm trying to prove to you that just because you *think* your memory is improving, doesn't mean it actually is. Everyone's already admitted lying to you – how do you know you're not lying to yourself?'

Dan sighed. 'Go on then.'

Brian went through Adams' usual questions, which Dan answered just as before – all except one.

'Who won the World Cup?'

Dan went quiet. He got off the bed. His pyjama jacket fell to the floor. He walked over to the sink and stared into the mirror above it. The question had made him remember something, but it wasn't the answer.

'Tony showed me a film of the final game this morning. We didn't watch it all the way through, because as soon as it started, I realised I'd seen it before and knew what the result was going to be.' He dropped his head. 'But not now.' He walked back to the bed and lay down on it. 'You told me yesterday I had to find a back road while I still could. Now I know what you meant.'

Brian moved closer to him. 'Dan, it's pretty clear. Whatever the reason we decided to stop taking the red pill, our memory is still deteriorating. If we can't retain something remembered just a few hours before, how long do you think it's going to be before memories of Lucy or Claire start going the same way?' He noticeably steeled himself before adding: 'How long before we forget them *completely*? We have to resume taking it – there is no alternative.'

Dan was about to agree but then sat up. 'Repeat all the questions.'

'What?'

'Ask me all the questions again.'

Dan got off the bed and went back to the sink. Brian furrowed his brow but did as asked. Dan answered everything as before while studying his face in the mirror. Brian asked about the World Cup, but Dan dismissed it – he was waiting for the last question.

'What happened in the aircraft crash?'

Dan raised a finger. He stood back from the basin, but continued looking into the mirror above it.

'What do all the previous questions have in common that's entirely absent from just that one?'

Brian shrugged.

Dan continued. 'I either know the answer or know *something about* the answer.' He looked at Brian. 'I know absolutely *nothing* about the answer to that one. Even my memory of a broken right arm and burning hand turned out to be from a barbecue accident here two weeks ago.'

Brian started to look lost. 'And your point is?'

'The point is, my dear brother – the reason why I can't remember anything about the crash is because *it never happened.*'

Brian flopped onto Dan's bed and put a hand to his head. 'Then how do you explain all the burns?'

'Exactly!'

Dan untied the draw-cord to his pyjama bottoms and let them drop to the floor. He viewed his naked body in the mirror. Brian looked anywhere but.

'The entire surface area of my body appears to have been horribly burnt, but it's impossible for anyone to survive one hundred per cent burns. Whatever caused this, it wasn't fire.'

He walked towards the mirror and prodded the flesh

on his face. 'Now, the question is, what did? What causes the *appearance* of burns?' He turned to Brian. 'And why doesn't it upset me any more?' He went back to the mirror. 'What's *really* happened to me and everyone else in this place?'

CHAPTER SIX

Dan stepped away from the mirror and turned around. He tried looking over his shoulder, but this hurt his neck too much. He presented his back to Brian.

'I assume I'm like this all over? The one hundred per cent burns theory falls down otherwise. What can you see?'

Brian kept looking elsewhere. 'I'm in your head, remember? I can only see what you see.' He stared up at the ceiling before adding: 'Unfortunately.'

Dan wondered how else to do it. 'I'll need to check all the other patients anyway, so I'll get one of them to look me over at the same time.'

Brian seemed to think he was joking. 'Really? And you think the best way to win friends and influence people is by asking them to take all their clothes off?'

Dan thought about the social difficulties. 'Hmmm. There's got to be a way. Without being certain everyone has the same all-over damage, the theory of the aircraft crash being a figment of my imagination is dead in the water.'

The door opened and a porter appeared with Gary in a wheelchair. Dan seized the opportunity.

'Ah, Gary. Good. Look at my bottom and tell me

what you think.' He turned his back and pointed at his buttocks.

Gary threw a thumb over his shoulder. 'Get me out of this madhouse.'

Without batting an eye, the porter reversed and pushed Gary back in the direction they had just come from. Undeterred, Dan followed them out.

'Gary, please. I want you to look at my bottom.' The porter outpaced Dan, who ended up standing starkers in the middle of the corridor. He made one last attempt. 'It's okay, I need to see you naked too.'

Dan found himself amongst spectators. He spotted Tracy striding her way through them. She didn't look happy – again. He retraced his steps, closed the door, and leaned on it. Brian had gone. *Coward*, he thought.

Tracy tried to enter the room. 'Let me in!'

'I can't.'

'Why not?'

'I'm not decent.'

Tracy released the door handle. 'What? And standing naked in the middle of the hospital is? Let me in!'

Dan kept the pressure on the door. 'I need to put some clothes on first.'

'Well, it's a pity you didn't think of that two minutes ago. Move away from the door NOW!'

Dan got into bed and pulled the covers up. She opened the door and stood there with her arms folded. Dan wondered if that was less severe than hands on hips. It wasn't.

'Just what the hell do you think you're playing at?'

'Nothing,' he said defensively.

Tracy closed the door. She swept his pyjamas up off the floor and proceeded to dress him.

She seemed to mellow a little. 'Dan, you can't walk around the hospital like that – what were you thinking?'

'I have a theory about why I can't remember the aircraft crash, and wanted to confirm it – that's all.'

'What? That you were flying in your birthday suit?'

'You enjoy treating me like a child, don't you? No, of course not.'

A moment of inspiration hit him and he grabbed her by the wrist. 'You've given me a bed bath. In fact, you must have given me numerous baths over the last six months – not to mention having to deal with things like bed sores.'

Tracy wrestled her wrist away. 'Of course I have.'

She went back to fastening the buttons on his jacket. He stopped her and pulled the front of it open.

'So, tell me. Am I like this all over?'

Tracy looked at him as if it were a test. 'More or less, why?'

Dan was finally getting somewhere. 'Would you go so far as to say, *every single square inch* of me looks like this?'

Tracy took control of his jacket again. 'Is this a trick question?'

Dan was on a roll. 'And are *all* the patients on this wing affected in *exactly* the same way?'

Tracy stood back. Her arms remained at her sides, which Dan took as a good sign. She still appeared wary, though.

'I take it there's a point to me stating the obvious?'

Dan checked the door was closed and then beckoned for her to move closer.

'What's the largest percentage of burns a person has ever been known to survive?'

Tracy raised her eyes as if searching for the answer. She appeared to find it. 'I don't know what the record is, but a casualty presenting with more than seventy to eighty per cent probably wouldn't survive.'

Dan sat back and grinned, satisfied. He became serious again. 'If I tell you what I know, will you tell Doctor Adams?'

Tracy widened her eyes, and exaggerated a slow nod of her head. 'Of course I'm going to pass on anything of significance to Doctor Adams. You're a patient in a hospital that specialises in neurological illnesses. Any memories you recall or form might be important to your recovery.'

Dan thought about that. He could keep his discovery to himself, but he needed to move on to the next stage, which was finding out what had actually caused the damage. He knew Tracy would in all likelihood either lie or go along with whatever he had to say anyway, because that's what his treatment demanded. He decided to take a chance.

'You can tell the good doctor,' he chose his next words carefully, 'I don't *think* I, or anybody else here, was involved in an aircraft accident.'

Tracy nodded, picked up his pyjama bottoms and offered them to him.

Dan was disappointed by her reaction. 'Don't you want to know how I came to that conclusion?'

Tracy grabbed his left foot and fed it into one of the trouser legs. 'Only if you want to tell me, but I assume your question about burn percentages has got something to do with it.'

Dan grabbed her wrist again. 'You know full well none of the patients here could possibly have been in a fire, so what caused this?' He held up the back of his left hand.

'Dan, are you going to tell me something else? Because if you are, I'm going to need pen and paper, otherwise I'll just forget.'

He became frustrated. 'You know *exactly* what did this, don't you?'

'Yes, I do, but if I tell you, you'll only turn it into a recovered memory and I'll get the sack for causing it. Sorry, Dan, but you're going to have to work it all out for yourself.'

Dan harrumphed. 'It's a conspiracy, if you ask me.'

'Well, that's the nature of the human brain, I'm afraid. If it can't think of a rational explanation, then why not give paranoia a try – even healthy people do that.'

She got his pyjama bottoms to his thighs and invited him to carry on. He pulled them up and retied the cord. There was a knock on the door and an orderly brought in his lunch.

Tracy glanced at the other bed. 'Looks like you've scared off your roommate.'

Dan decided there was an upside to his latest

contretemps with Gary after all. 'Yes, that's a pity – very unfortunate.'

She scowled. 'I'm sure we can find a replacement.'

He scowled back. Tracy turned to leave.

'Nothing else you want to add before I go?'

Dan couldn't think of anything, so Tracy left. Dan began idly picking at the contents of his lunch tray while musing what to do next. Brian appeared on the other bed.

'Is it my imagination or has Tracy lost weight?'

Dan ignored him. He was going through an imaginary list of accidents other than fire that could cause burns. Brian carried on about Tracy.

'Whatever it is, she looks a lot healthier – prettier even.'

Dan was thinking of a list of chemicals that could produce acid burns when he picked up on what Brian was saying. He put down the sandwich and made his way into the corridor to see if Tracy was still there. She was chatting with a colleague some twenty feet away. She had her back to him, but he could see enough to get where Brian was coming from.

The rolls of fat Dan had so judgementally observed the day before seemed to have all but disappeared. They were still there, but only just. The difference was remarkable given the time interval. Her legs looked longer too and for a moment he thought she must be wearing the stilettos he used to fantasise about – but no, still the same flats. He went back into the room and closed the door.

Brian continued while Dan pondered the perceived transformation. 'Maybe she's got a new boyfriend or just dumped one. Women have a habit of being able to transform themselves under those circumstances.'

'I must have been mistaken yesterday. She looks as if she's lost a good two stone in weight since then, but there's no way that can happen overnight.'

Dan put the idea out of his mind and went back to pondering a list of corrosive substances. 'Maybe we were all involved in some kind of industrial accident,' he speculated to himself.

Brian changed the subject. 'There is something else we might have to come to terms with if we're right about the aircraft crash never happening.' He sat up. 'Maybe we're not a pilot? Maybe we're not even a squadron leader in the RAF?'

Dan stopped thinking about chemical factories and burst out laughing.

Brian folded his arms. 'Listen, if you're going to mock everything I say, then at least have the decency to think through it first. Give me one good reason why you *must* be a pilot.'

Dan managed to control himself. He wiped a tear from his eye. 'Okay, okay, Brian.' He tried to be serious. 'If I'm not a pilot in the RAF, then what am I?'

Brian looked a little foolish. He cast his eyes down at the floor and drew an imaginary circle on it with his foot. 'I don't know. A factory worker maybe?'

Dan stared at his hallucination. 'Brian, do I look like the kind of person who has to labour for a living?' He sneered before chuckling at that nonsense too.

'Okay then. If the crash never happened, then that

explains why we can't remember the type of aircraft involved – because there wasn't one.' He challenged Dan. 'But I assume you can name the different types of aircraft we *have* flown?'

'Of course I can.' Dan sat up and put out the fingers of his left hand to reel them off. Except that he couldn't. He stopped seeing the ridiculous in Brian's suggestion and became quiet. Dan dismissed the question with a shake of the head. 'I've temporarily forgotten them – that's all. Just like I temporarily forgot England won the World Cup.'

They pointed at each other and shouted in unison. 'I'VE REMEMBERED!' They tried to celebrate by shaking each other's hand, but ended up grasping at thin air instead. Dan picked up his sandwich and took a bite to congratulate himself that way.

'Don't worry, Brian, the aircraft will soon come back to me. It's just a matter of time.'

He hoped the same could be said for the rest of his flying career, as he couldn't remember any of that either. He wouldn't admit it, but he couldn't even recall being in the military, let alone a squadron leader in the Royal Air Force. He just knew he was. He had to be.

Dan lay back on the bed to think about chemical factories, when he found himself standing in the middle of one. He must have fallen asleep. He knew he was dreaming this time, though. Dan was surrounded by giant silos with different chemical formulae printed on the sides in large letters like H_2SO_4, HNO_3, and HCI. All of them were highly corrosive and he waited for one to burst open so he could identify the real cause of the burns. Nothing happened. *Brian's got to be here somewhere*, he thought. He shouted out his brother's name a few times, but it just echoed around the cavernous building.

Dan could see and hear a machine being operated further within the factory so decided to investigate, all the time expecting at least one of the silos to erupt and cover him in acid. The thought wasn't particularly concerning, as Dan figured he would just wake up. To his disappointment, it didn't happen. He approached what appeared to be factory workers carrying out the duties of whatever the plant's purpose was. As with the previous dream, Dan didn't recognise any of them, but thought he should. Their activities concentrated on a large conveyor belt running through the centre of the building.

There were various bits of old machinery, like washing machines, vacuum cleaners, fridges, filing cabinets, and even cars, being conveyed along the belt. The factory seemed to be a disposal or recycling centre. One of the workers offered Dan the red pill. He refused it. The worker looked disappointed, but neither persisted nor insisted, and went back to whatever he'd been doing.

Dan recognised some of the items on the conveyor belt as aircraft components, and it dawned on him that perhaps the purpose of the dream was to remember the type of plane he flew. He followed the belt alongside in the hope of identifying them, passing some workers along the way. They each tried to get him to take the red pill, but he ignored them all.

The aircraft parts were getting away, so Dan leapt up onto the conveyor belt and picked his way forward through the other bits of scrap to get to them. The belt was heading towards a crusher, and Dan calculated he would be waking up in around thirty seconds. He grabbed a wing flap and turned it over in his hands, looking for a clue to its origin. He was about to drop it and pick up a cockpit instrument when he heard the familiar sound of a filing cabinet drawer being opened.

He looked up to see Brian taking a folder from it and straight away Dan recognised it as aircraft documentation. He called out for Brian to pass the folder but to Dan's frustration, Brian did the same as the last dream: indicated he didn't want to be disturbed. Dan looked past Brian and, realising the dream was about to end in seconds, lunged forward and grabbed the file. Brian kept hold of it and they entered into a tug of war.

'Give me the file, Brian.'

Dan's eyes flicked back and forth between the crusher and his brother. Brian shook his head. Five seconds to go, but Dan only needed to glance at the contents to get what he wanted.

'Give me the file. NOW!'

Less than two seconds, but Brian was still holding firm.

'I SAID, GIVE IT TO ME!'

Adams looked at Dan. 'I'm afraid I can't.'

Dan was holding one end of a notepad. The hand at

the other end belonged to his doctor. Dan glanced at the empty bed opposite. Satisfied he was now awake, he let go.

'Do you know who I am?'

The usual questions were then reeled off and much to Dan's relief, he managed to answer them all – including the one about the World Cup. He guessed Tracy would have informed the doctor about the aircraft crash being a figment of his imagination, so stuck to his guns and repeated the same. The doctor just seemed to accept it. But then he would react in the same way if told fairies lived at the bottom of Dan's garden. For all Dan knew, he may even have said that.

Dan became sheepish. 'I've answered the question about the World Cup correctly before and then forgotten it, haven't I?'

The doctor nodded.

Dan cleared his throat. 'I think I may also have mentioned something about...' He felt silly saying it, but knew if he didn't, it would only bug him. 'Fairies? Fairies, er, living at the bottom of my garden?'

Adams stopped writing. 'You were just making a point. It was clear you didn't actually believe that.'

Dan breathed a sigh of relief.

'The good news is you're starting to recognise the vulnerability of your short-term memory as well as the long-term. The bad news is they will both get worse unless you restart your medication.'

Adams pointed at what was on the bedside table. Dan sneered at it.

'Tell you what, Doc, I'll take your pill if you tell me what caused this.'

He tapped his face with a finger. The doctor replied with a question.

'Why did you decide to stand naked in the corridor yesterday?'

With a mixture of exasperation and embarrassment, Dan explained the method behind the apparent madness and waited for Doctor Adams to give his usual reply. He managed to synchronise it with him.

'Interesting,' they both said, simultaneously.

It made Dan feel a bit better, even though the doctor didn't seem to notice – deliberately or otherwise.

Adams ended his visit with some administrative concerns. 'Are you happy with your new accommodation?'

Dan surveyed the room. 'Haven't I always been here?'

The doctor made another entry on his notepad and left. Dan assumed the answer to his question must have been 'No'.

Brian was looking at himself in the mirror. Dan leapt at him, but ended up on the other bed instead.

'Idiot! Why didn't you let go of the folder?'

Brian didn't answer. He placed a finger under one eye and drew the lid down. 'Do I look old to you?'

Dan ignored the question.

'There were aircraft parts on that conveyor belt and you were holding the documentation to them. All I had to do was look at it and I would have remembered at least one of the aircraft types I flew! Why didn't you let me have it?'

Brian took his hand away from his face and glared at him. 'Dan, how many times do I have to remind you that we are one and the same? In other words, what I see, you see, and vice versa. Had you not decided to try and grab the folder from me, then there would have been plenty of time for me, or should I say *us*, to read it, and we would now be very much the wiser.'

He went back to studying his face. Dan put his head in his hands. Much as he hated to admit it, he had to agree.

'Okay, from now on, when I, er, I mean *we* dream, we don't interfere with whatever the other is doing.'

'And in reality.'

Dan looked puzzled.

'It doesn't matter whether you see me here or in a dream, I'm exactly the same – a figment conjured up by our brain to help make sense of things. Any conflict between the two of us here could be just as detrimental.' He peered into the mirror more closely. 'Maybe worse.'

Dan was demoralised, so Brian tried cheering him up. 'Look, we've had two dreams now, each one an attempt to sort out the mess that's our brain. There must be something we can take away from them.'

Dan groaned. 'I can't see what. The first ended with a mug of tea being thrust at me, and the second with a notepad being pulled away. Make of that what you will.'

Brian walked over to the window and surveyed the scene below. 'There has to be a common factor. Something the dreams share.'

Dan was still disheartened. 'The first was outdoors

and the second in a factory. Even the people were different – we were the only common factor.'

'No, you and I are a given. We're after a detail common to both.'

Dan got off the bed and joined Brian. He resumed his analysis. 'Well, the snow turned out to be letters of the alphabet and there were letters on the silos in the factory.' He stopped. 'And you took a folder out of a filing cabinet. We've been talking a lot about filing cabinets recently.'

An E-type Jaguar drove into view. Brian grinned and changed the subject. 'Wow. Look at that. Something else we've always dreamt about, eh?'

The driver parked the car beneath the window.

Dan didn't know if the letters and files in the dreams were connected, but they were in the reality of a hospital.

Tony got out of the car, which wiped the smile off Brian's face.

'How can Tony afford a car like that?'

Dan didn't care. He now knew where to find the answer to what had happened to him and everyone else. He watched Tony enter the building and hatched a plan to ensure he got access to the hospital's patient files.

It wasn't going to be blackmail – more like revenge. Revenge for having an affair with his wife. Dan seethed. He was about to receive a visit from someone he thought was a close friend, only to seen him kiss his wife full on the lips just the day before. Dan was so angry he wondered if he would even be able to control himself while presenting Tony with the fait accompli: Claire and he could have what they wanted providing Dan got Lucy and proof of what had happened to him and the other patients.

Like it or not, Tony would have to get access to the hospital's records. Dan flinched with pain as he clenched his fists in a mixture of rage and nervous anticipation. He only had to hit Tony once and any chance of the plan working would be over. No matter what, Dan had to remain calm throughout while his demands were detailed. There was a knock on the door and Tony walked in. He threw what he had in his arms onto the bed.

'Right, get dressed. We're getting out of this place for a while.'

Dan looked at the clothes. He wanted to say something, but couldn't remember what it was.

'Are you all right?'

Dan frowned. 'There was something I had to say to you.' He tried to recall it. 'But I've forgotten what it was.'

Tony smiled. 'Let's get you dressed – I think you're going to like what I have waiting for you outside.' Dan undid the buttons on his pyjamas while wondering what it could be.

A few minutes later and Dan was being wheeled down the corridor towards the hospital lifts. He pressed the button when they got there.

'Tony? Do you and I need to discuss anything? Something of a personal nature?'

His friend became furtive and glanced up and down the corridor. He raised a finger to his lips. 'Shhh. Not here. Wait till we're outside.'

At least Dan knew it was something important. They descended in the lift and were soon in the open air, admiring Dan's dream car – an E-type Jaguar.

'When did you get this? Must have cost a fortune. Brand new too, looking at the number plate.'

'You're joking, aren't you? I can't afford this – thought it might help with your memory.'

Dan's face lit up. 'You mean I own this? This is my car?'

'Come on, Dan. You should know the score by now. You tell me what you genuinely believe and I'll nod my head and pretend to agree.'

Dan scowled at him. 'Yeah, that's one thing I do remember – my family and friends have all turned on me in the name of my so-called recovery.'

Tony shrugged. 'Do you want to go for a spin, or what?'

Dan became like the proverbial kid in a sweet shop and hauled himself out of the wheelchair by the door handle. Tony squeezed the chair into the E-type's boot.

They were soon hurtling down country lanes. Dan was enjoying the ride, but a sense of escaping the hospital surpassed it. He inspected and ran his hands over every surface within reach, waiting for something to trigger what he hoped for – that the car was his. It didn't happen.

'Perhaps if I drove for a bit?'

Tony laughed. 'Not a hope in hell's chance. Not

insured for a start, and Lucy would never forgive me if I didn't bring her dad back in one piece.'

The mention of his daughter made Dan think she was what they had to discuss, but he couldn't think why. Trees and hedgerows flashed by.

'Everything seems so green compared to how I remember it.'

Tony slowed as they approached a layby. 'That's because you've been stuck in that hospital for six months. The last time you saw trees and hedges, most of them would have been bare.' He indicated, pulled over, and switched off the engine. 'Right.' He reached behind Dan's seat. 'Feast your eyes on that lot.'

Paperwork landed on Dan's lap. It appeared to be photocopies of something, but the print was blurred. 'What's this?'

'What you asked me to get you months ago – patient records.'

Dan suddenly remembered that was part of what he wanted Tony to do. The word sunk in. 'Months? I asked for these *months* ago?'

'Almost since the day you first woke up. It's taken me all this time to gain access and copy them. Just call me Bond – *James Bond*.'

Dan chuckled. 'You should have brought an Aston Martin instead.' He became serious. 'You won't get into trouble, will you?'

Tony tapped the side of his nose. 'Ask no questions and I'll tell you no lies.'

Dan raised his eyebrows. 'Well, that's debatable.

Particularly as deceit from others appears to be a necessary part of my treatment.' He held the first copy up and then brought it to his nose. It remained blurred. Dan dropped it back to his lap. A scan of the rest revealed them all to be just as bad. 'Well, I'm sorry, Bond, but you've screwed up. They're impossible to read.' Dan coudn't hide his frustration.

Tony reached into the glove compartment.

'Here, put your reading glasses on.'

Dan looked at him as if he had two heads. 'Glasses? Tony, I'm a pilot – I don't need glasses.'

Tony insisted. 'Try them anyway.'

Dan squinted in disdain before sliding them on. Everything within newspaper-print reading range snapped into focus. He took them off. 'How long have I needed to wear these?'

Tony tapped the side of his nose again.

Dan put the glasses back on and read the cover of the first file. 'All the names and addresses have been blanked out.'

Tony regarded Dan as if he'd been born yesterday. 'Of course they have. My, er, "contact" wouldn't let me copy them otherwise. Anyway, I thought you just wanted to know what happened to you all, not who'd make the most suitable bridge partner.'

Dan agreed. He read to himself, but made the odd comment out loud. 'Boring. Not interested. Not applicable. Too minor.'

He tutted before placing the folder under the pile and starting on the next one. Tony put a hand on top of it.

'Wait a minute – what did you get from that guy? I assume he's male.'

Dan pulled the files away from Tony. 'I don't know, it didn't say. Talked more about what he can and can't do now, rather than what caused him to be admitted in the first place. Very frustrating.' He continued reading, but was soon shaking his head. He speed-read through the next two files. 'This is pointless. They only mention how patients are responding to the treatment – nothing I don't already know. Have you read these?'

Tony nodded. Dan dropped the files back onto his lap.

'Then do they say what actually caused the burns?'

'Sorry, Dan. You know I'm not allowed to put answers straight into your head. Nothing wrong with sowing the seeds, though – hence this car and those files. I hate to sound like Doctor Adams, but there's a good reason why you have to work it all out for yourself.'

Dan sighed. He was getting fed up with everyone knowing what had happened, except him. 'I assume there is still a point to reading these?'

Dan took Tony's indifference as a yes, and continued to study the documents. He spoke again after a minute or so.

'There are injuries and the causes of them mentioned, but only in reference to accidents suffered *after* admission.' He pondered that. 'Which file's mine?'

Tony flicked through the pile and pulled out the one marked with a cross. Dan skipped through it until he found what he was looking for.

Everything about his accident with the barbecue was detailed word for word and as he remembered it, but something about the author's conclusion intrigued him. He gave it to Tony and told him to keep the page open while he found and read findings from two similar incidents. He drew attention to them.

'Listen to this: "The inquiry found the condition caused him to trip."' He read out loud from another file. '"The condition led to the fall."' He took his file back from Tony and emphasised the operative word. '"The *condition* caused him to stumble and put his left hand into the flames."' He turned to Tony. 'We're all suffering from some kind of medical condition, aren't we?'

Tony started the engine.

CHAPTER SEVEN

Dan studied the backs of his hands. 'So, what is it then?'

Tony switched on the car's indicator and prepared to pull out. 'Fancy some breakfast?'

Dan knew Tony was avoiding the question, but was hungry all the same.

The E-type was manoeuvred back out on to the road. There was nothing ahead so Tony put his foot down and, within seconds, had exceeded the speed limit. He kept on accelerating.

The E-type had just passed seventy miles per hour when Dan realised the glasses enabled him to see his injuries in greater detail, so he brought both hands up to his face. Eighty came and went.

'I suppose burns could technically still be defined as a condition.'

Ninety. The uneven road surface caused his hands to jump, but he worked through it.

'But no one can survive one hundred per cent burns, so it *can't* be that.'

One hundred. The car began to gently pitch up and down. Dan continued to study his hands.

'And there's the psychological issues. *Everyone* has them in one form or another.'

One hundred and ten. The car crested bumps as opposed to absorbing them. Even with his glasses, increasing vibration meant Dan's hands became a blur, so he dropped them back onto his lap.

'And we're all in a hospital that specialises in neurology.'

The needle passed through one hundred and twenty miles per hour and Tony grinned – just as a tractor drove out of a field and into their path. Tony stamped on the brakes and attempted to steer around it but the wheels had locked and the E-type started to slide. The car drifted, with just the bonnet making it to the overtaking side of the road. The passenger compartment was less than a second away from hitting the rear-right quarter of the tractor when one of the rear wheels dug into a pot-hole and, by a miracle, bounced the car back into line.

They hurtled past, clearing the machine by inches. Another miracle ensured no vehicles were approaching in the opposite direction, otherwise they'd both be dead by now. Tony took his foot off the brake, pulled back over to the correct side of the road and coasted into a layby. He switched off the engine.

Dan turned to him. 'We're all suffering from some kind of *psychological* condition, aren't we?'

Tony snapped. 'Didn't you see the tractor? We nearly hit it!'

Dan was unmoved. He looked at the trembling

hands on the steering wheel. 'Shouldn't I be asking *you* that question?'

'Well, yes, but even so, how can you just take it so calmly? We could have been killed!'

Dan remained impassive. 'It's no big deal. I'd just wake up.'

Tony turned to Dan and put a hand on his forearm. 'Dan – we're not in a dream – this is reality! We were doing well over a hundred miles an hour. Had we collided with that tractor, we'd both be dead now.' He leaned across. '*For real.*'

Dan stared ahead and put a hand to his temple.

The tractor pulled up behind and the driver ran over. 'Are you two all right?'

Tony wound down the window to answer, but nervous shock caused him to fumble the response. 'Fine thanks! Lovely tractor. What'll she do?'

The farmer said nothing – he was watching the passenger slamming the lid of the glove compartment against his fingers. Dan let out a yelp, and placed the bruised digits under the opposite armpit. He grimaced while acknowledging the tractor driver.

'It's okay, I thought we were dreaming!'

The farmer mumbled, 'Bloody idiots' and went back to his tractor. He climbed into it and went on his way. He mouthed something as he drove past.

Tony gulped some fresh air through the open window. Dan rubbed his hand.

'Well, you may as well certify me now. Hallucinations, amnesia, and paranoia are one thing, but when you start thinking real life is a dream, there really is no hope.'

'When did you start thinking you were dreaming?'

Dan thought back over that morning's events. 'The second you threw my clothes on the bed, I guess. I had something important I wanted to say, but completely forgot it. I only remembered what it was when you gave me the patient files in the layby, so assumed I must have fallen asleep when you walked into the room.' He looked at his friend. 'Are you feeling okay?'

'I think so. What about you? Has escaping what should have been our certain deaths sunk in yet?'

Dan indicated it had, but only because he assumed it would at any moment.

Tony appeared to recover. 'Well, I'm glad I didn't let you drive. I can hear it now: "It's okay, Tony, I'll keep accelerating into the back of that tractor and we'll just wake up!"' They both smiled but only to reassure each other. The engine was restarted. 'Let's get some breakfast.'

A couple of sedate miles later and Tony pulled into a roadside café. He climbed out and went to retrieve the wheelchair from the boot. He was shaky on his feet. It made Dan realise he still didn't feel the slightest bit bothered by the narrowness of their escape. There was no doubt about it – the car was out of control and going at a speed that would have killed them both instantly had they hit the tractor.

He thought about the finality of that. It didn't move him at all. 'Maybe I want to die.' Dan dismissed the idea, but not before acknowledging it wasn't the first time the subject of suicide had been raised.

A short while later and they'd recovered enough to enjoy two fried breakfasts. Empty plates lay between them. Dan looked out of the window at the E-type.

'So, how fast will it go?'

Tony put down his mug of tea. 'One hundred and fifty, theoretically. Although I think that was achieved on a trial with a specially modified car.' He eyed Dan suspiciously. 'Don't even think about going that fast on the way back.'

Dan smiled. 'It's funny how we're never satisfied with what we have. That car was built to be the best there is and yet there's always someone who wants it to be better. Faster. More fuel-efficient. Imagine if we treated people the same way.'

Tony reached for the tea pot. 'We do, if you think about it. There's always some new medical advance to make you live longer.' He pointed at Dan. 'You're a classic example.'

Tony refilled his mug and Dan's spirits lifted – he hoped what had happened to him and the others was about to be revealed. It wasn't.

'Without the regular testing of new drugs and procedures, you'd be dead by now – it's as simple as that.'

Dan tried not to look too disappointed. He put on his glasses and studied his hands again. 'Just tell me I'm going to wake up one day and all this will be back to normal.'

'Still think you're in a dream?'

Dan's response was instant. 'No – a nightmare.'

Tony adopted a look that Dan had seen enough of by now to know his friend's next statement would either be a manipulated truism or an outright lie. Dan was still surprised by it, though.

'I *guarantee* you'll be back to normal.'

Tony sat back. He looked a bit too pleased with himself for Dan's liking.

'Sorry to sound ungrateful, Tony, but I'd rather hear that from someone a bit more qualified.'

'Doctor Adams would say exactly the same.'

'I very much doubt it and, even if he did, it would just be a ruse to get me to restart the medication he's so fond of.' Dan's eyes glazed over. 'Why was I even *allowed* to refuse the red pill?'

Tony didn't answer and rotated the bezel of his watch unnecessarily.

Dan regarded the E-type again. He thought of what had been done to increase its speed. 'Am I involved in some kind of clinical trial?'

Tony still said nothing.

Dan pressed the issue. 'Is the red pill experimental? That would certainly explain why I had the choice to refuse it – it's yet to be certified for general use. But why all the cloak and dagger nonsense? I don't believe for one second it's to ensure my memories are "real".' He turned that over in his head before coming to a conclusion. 'It's classified, isn't it?'

Tony looked at his watch. 'We'd better get going.'

Dan laughed.

'What's so funny?'

'I was just thinking how worried I was about divulging the clandestine nature of my non-existent flying mission, and yet here I am, in the middle of a *real* government cover-up.'

Tony checked to see if anyone was listening. Dan stopped chuckling. 'Are the two connected in some way?'

Tony looked at his watch again. Dan reached out and put a hand over it.

'They are, aren't they?'

Tony pulled his hand away, took some cash out of his wallet and left it on the table.

The journey back commenced in silence. Dan glanced across at the speedometer which was reading a not-unsurprising fifty miles per hour. He broke the silence.

'Let's play a game – I'll tell you what I think is going on and all you have to do is say nothing to confirm it or make something up to prove I'm still right.'

Tony didn't respond to the light-hearted attempt at getting to the truth. He appeared to be uncomfortable. Dan made a start on his thesis.

'I don't think I or anybody else has been in an accident that causes burns – fire or chemical.'

Tony fixed his eyes on the road while Dan continued.

'I think what we're actually suffering from is the *condition* referred to in the patient files.'

Tony remained silent, although a constant change of grip on the steering wheel betrayed a need to be somewhere else.

'The hospital specialises in neurology, so the condition must be psychological.'

Still no response.

'Some kind of mental condition that not only causes hallucinations, amnesia, and paranoia, but can also make dreams appear real and reality an illusion.' He pulled down his sun visor and looked in the mirror. 'It even has the power to make us *think* we all have burns and other accident injuries which, in my case, were the result of an imaginary aircraft crash.'

Tony kept his poker face. Dan moved from logic to speculation.

'Now. Does this mean the trial of the red pill is going according to plan, or has it gone disastrously wrong?' He peered at Tony – still nothing. 'I'm willing to bet it's the latter, which is why I chose to stop taking it. That would explain why I'm not so horrified by my appearance any more. It's improving because now I've ceased the medication, the psychosis it causes is subsiding. You even told me just now you could *guarantee* my recovery back to normal. By refusing to take the pill, I've effectively taken myself off the trial, so that's bound to happen.'

Tony remained impassive.

'The question is: what was the pill *supposed* to do?' Dan thought more about their conversation at breakfast. 'You also said: "There's always some new medical advance to make you live longer." Is that what this is all about? Is that what the pill was meant to do, and now that it's all gone wrong the hospital is keen to keep a lid on it?'

Tony pulled the car over and stopped. Without saying a word, he got out and walked a few paces further up the road. He lit a cigarette.

Dan wondered if he was a smoker and had forgotten that too.

Tony took a couple of deep puffs before walking back to the passenger side of the car. He motioned Dan to wind down the window before finally breaking his silence.

'Have you had any thoughts of suicide or felt you'd be perfectly happy to die?'

Dan tried not to look shocked at the question and lied. 'No, why?'

Tony walked another few yards in the opposite direction. Dan adjusted the rear-view mirror to see Tony inhale two more puffs. The suicide question and Dan's subsequent denial of it made him nervous, but not as much as Tony clearly was. He returned to the car and got in.

'The red pill *is* experimental and you are all involved in a clinical trial.' Tony restarted the engine. 'But it's not what you think it is.'

They continued their journey. But for the suicide question, Dan would have punched the air. He tried to appear nonchalant about it.

'Why did you ask me if I'd had any thoughts of suicide?'

Tony sang like a canary. Whatever had held his tongue for the last few miles didn't seem to matter any more or, if it did, he didn't care.

'You all have a psychological condition the red pill is designed to cure.' He corrected Dan. 'And it *is* working.' Tony focussed his attention back to the road ahead. 'The trouble is, before patients get better, it exacerbates the original illness, to the point where some kind of paranoid schizophrenia gives rise to obsessive thoughts of suicide.' He reached across, grabbed Dan's arm by the cast and lifted it to his face. 'What were your immediate thoughts when you first saw your hands?'

Dan didn't need to think twice. 'I wanted to die.'

'And have you had similar thoughts since?'

Dan wondered if he should come clean, but decided to maintain the lie. 'No.'

Tony hadn't finished. 'The scary thing is, patients actually become comfortable with thoughts of suicide, to the extent they genuinely believe it's a *natural* thing to do.'

It was Dan's turn to remain silent. Tony appeared to change the subject.

'Has your hallucination said anything?'

Dan was confused. 'Brian? What about him?'

'Hallucinations can act as a kind of comfort blanket during the healing process. Something like a close friend, favourite uncle – even a toy the patient was once close to. The problem is that the support mechanism backfires spectacularly if it ends up encouraging suicide instead.'

Dan looked over his shoulder. Brian made a hand gesture to show he thought Tony was the one with the psychological condition.

'Brian's been fine. Very supportive of my recovery, actually.'

Tony was still concerned. 'Just be prepared for him to be supportive in a different way if you start seeing suicide as a natural way out of your illness.'

Dan was staggered at just how natural the feeling was. He knew the moment he first saw the tractor he would have been happy to die then – even with the thought of leaving behind a wife and daughter he loved very much. In fact, they were the only thing that stopped him from grabbing the steering wheel and ending it all right now – Dan wanted to ensure their physical and financial security first.

Brian leaned forward and whispered in Dan's ear. 'Don't worry, mate. I won't let you go until that's sorted.'

Dan felt reassured by that, but knew Tony would be horrified.

'So, if the pill's a success and not a failure, why all the subterfuge? Why not just tell patients thoughts of suicide are a side-effect that needs to be managed while they recover?'

'I'm no shrink, but my guess is you don't tell someone about to jump off a bridge to manage their situation. You either grab them, distract them or both. From what I understand, the hospital's version of that is to keep you all under close supervision, while encouraging your thoughts to take an interest elsewhere.'

Tony explained why Dan had been lied to from day one. 'The condition causes confusion, memory loss, and suspicion anyway – throw a few half-truths and lies in and you've got the perfect recipe for a conspiracy to develop. A patient obsessing with that is infinitely preferable to one planning a suicide.'

It seemed plausible, but Dan still wasn't convinced. 'Isn't there a danger that that could actually increase thoughts of suicide?'

'There is, but crucially, it buys time for the red pill to do its stuff, so hopefully things don't get that far.'

Dan's paranoia made sure he was suspicious of Tony's motives. 'Why have you suddenly decided to tell me all this? You could easily have remained silent on the way back to the hospital and I'd be none the wiser.'

Tony laughed. 'What I say or do is academic, because you'll just assume it's part of the conspiracy or forget everything I say anyway.' He glanced at Dan. 'My money's on the latter.'

Dan said nothing and waited for Tony to answer the question. 'Because I now realise there's an unknown issue with you – you're the only patient to refuse the red pill. That wasn't thought to be a problem as far as suicidal thoughts are concerned – coming off it should theoretically reduce them, but the incident with the tractor earlier, and your indifference to it, now that's something I'm pretty sure is new.'

Tony became more serious. 'Suppose turning reality into a dream is just another way for your mind to convince you to end it all *subconsciously*? Supposing you had been driving the car? Whatever the side-effects of the red pill, I think we need to convince you to start taking it again and as soon as possible. If that means telling you the truth from now on, then so be it.' He smiled weakly at Dan. 'Even if it does mean you'll forget all about it five minutes later.'

It all made sense, but Dan was still sceptical. 'Okay, but I want to be there when you repeat everything you've just said to Doctor Adams.'

Tony shrugged. 'Suits me.'

They arrived back at the hospital and Dan felt well enough to make his own way from the car park. Tracy was waiting when they got to his room.

'There you are. Take these.'

She held up Dan's daily pill quota and, after checking the red pill wasn't hiding somewhere, he swallowed them. There was something striking about Tracy's appearance, and Dan was about to ask if she was wearing make-up, when Doctor Adams walked through the door.

Tony was keen to discuss what had been said in the car, but the doctor was typically aloof and raised a hand. The standard questions were then reeled off to Dan. He thought he'd responded to them all correctly, but was stumped by an event that apparently ended with a window being broken. Adams made his usual notes before turning to Tony.

'Is there something you wish to add?'

True to his word, Tony repeated everything as promised. The doctor's eyes widened with disapproval, but his expression changed when details of the tractor incident were revealed. Adams closed the door.

'You lied to Tony about not feeling suicidal any more, didn't you?'

Dan was ashamed at having deceived his friend. 'I'm really sorry, Tony, but I was desperate to know everything and was afraid you'd just clam up again.'

If Tony felt betrayed, he didn't show it. He implored the doctor. 'But how can that be? Dan ceased taking his medication weeks ago. Surely the thoughts of suicide should be reducing? Can't you do something?'

The doctor was busy writing. He finished.

'I'm afraid we're going to have to put you on suicide watch.'

The sound of that worried Dan. 'What does that entail?'

'Nothing too onerous – you won't be allowed to leave the hospital and an orderly will be posted outside your door.' He looked at Tony. 'You're right. This is something new. Nobody else involved in the trial has ever thought reality was a dream – not even the control group.'

Both Dan and Tony said it in unison. 'Control group?'

Adams explained. 'All medical trials involve a separate group of patients with the same medical condition being given a placebo instead of the test drug. Everything else is the same. It's done so the outcome can be more accurately judged. If both group results are identical, then we know the drug has no effect, but if the experiment group shows improvement, then it must be successful.

'That said, there's obviously something different going on with a test subject who ceases to take the drug halfway through the trial, and we need to investigate that.' He softened his tone. 'I would have preferred to continue with encouraging you to recover your own thoughts, but given what Tony has described, that would be pointless now.'

Adams moved closer to Dan and picked up the red pill he'd left on the bedside table. 'I've always encouraged you to restart taking this because you were making good progress with it, but you're under no obligation to continue if you don't want to. However, given the incident with the tractor and your contentment with thoughts of your own death, I think it's imperative you restart the medication as soon as possible.'

Dan regarded the pill with disdain before shaking his head.

Adams lowered his voice. 'Dan, I think you should be prepared for your thoughts and visions to become further disconnected from reality. I'm not certain, but by discontinuing the red pill when you did, the increase in temporary psychosis it causes has not only been maintained, but is clearly worsening.'

He placed the pill back on the bedside table. 'You've always wanted honesty, so I'll make it as plain as I can. Unless you resume your medication, you're highly likely to experience the worst horrors the mind can conjure.' His lean towards Dan appeared to be calculated this time. 'And whatever you *think* that may be, it's nothing compared to what a *dying* brain can produce.'

Dan ignored him. He was thinking of how best to ready his estate for Claire and Lucy to inherit. He responded. 'I know you all have my best interests at heart, but please believe me when I say I've made up my mind – I'm happy for nature to take its course. If that means I make a full recovery then so be it, but whatever the outcome, I'm certain I no longer want to be part of the trial. I'd be grateful if arrangements could be made for my discharge, so I can be with my family again.'

They all looked at each other. Adams explained the reality of that.

'I'm afraid you can't. The reason why you were suitable for the trial in the first place was because your mental condition made it impossible for you to lead a normal life.'

Dan snapped at him. *'Then all the more reason to end it.'* He addressed Tony next. 'Can you get me a solicitor? I think I'm going to need one.'

Tony didn't respond. Tracy wiped away a tear. The doctor broke the short silence that followed.

'I'll be in first thing tomorrow morning to see how you feel.'

Dan scoffed at the implication he might have changed his mind by then – the inability of others to understand his position irritated him. They left Dan on his own, but the door remained open and, a short while later, an orderly posted himself in the corridor just outside. Dan tutted.

Brian appeared. 'Is he going to sit there all the time?'

The rediscovery of a piece of bacon wedged between his teeth made Dan wander over to the sink.

'God knows. I wish I'd carried on lying now. It's not as if I desperately want to end it all straight away – there's too much to sort out with Claire and Lucy first.' He picked up the toothbrush and toothpaste.

Brian seemed worried, but not for Dan or himself. 'How are we going to break it to them?'

Dan dwelled on that for a moment. 'Claire will understand, but Lucy won't. Tony will make a good father, though.'

He was about to put the brush into his mouth when he remembered what had caused the window to break. He grasped the sink with both hands as the recollection filled him with rage. He was about to re-enact the scene that led up to the champagne bottle being thrown when he calmed. Dan sighed at the irony.

'And to think I wanted to kill Tony this morning, when he's just about the most important friend a man could have – someone to seamlessly take over when I'm gone.'

Dan cleaned his teeth. Brian looked into the mirror over his shoulder. Dan was struck by their similar appearance. Even through his injuries – imagined or not – they could almost be twins.

Brian was still worried. 'Are we sure we're doing the right thing? I mean, I know it feels okay and makes perfect sense, but nobody else seems to see it our way.'

Dan spat into the basin. 'They'll get used to it.' He reached for the soap. 'They'll have to.'

Brian went from concern to discomfort. 'I suppose we ought to think about how we're actually going to do it.'

Dan plugged the basin and ran a tap. 'We'll cross that bridge when we get to it.' He looked at Brian in the mirror again. 'And jump off before we reach the other side.'

He smiled wryly, but Brian didn't. 'Some people would say we need our heads examined.'

Dan splashed water onto his face.

'Did you hear what I said?' Brian seemed to want to make a point.

Dan had heard him, but didn't respond as he was busy washing his face.

Brian repeated it. 'I said: some people would say we need to examine our heads.'

Dan brought some water up to wash his scalp and was about to pedantically correct the subtle difference between the two statements when his fingertips ran over what felt like dents. Eyes still closed, he slowed his movements and took a moment to identify how many, and where. He blindly reached for a towel and dried his eyes.

Dan opened them just as Brian brought his chin down to his chest. His head was scarred by a series of evenly spaced indentations.

CHAPTER EIGHT

'How many can you see?'

'Dan, how many times do I have to tell you – I can only see what you can.'

Dan lifted his chin off his chest. 'What's the point of having a helpful hallucination that doesn't help?' He went back to the mirror and ran his hands over his head for the umpteenth time. 'Well, I can see four, but I reckon there's eight in total. What do you think they are?'

Brian got up and looked over Dan's shoulder into the mirror again. 'Pretty obvious, I would have thought. Some kind of post-operative scarring. We've been under the knife for something.'

Dan furthered a second possibility. 'They could be an illusion – like the rest of the injuries.' He put his glasses on and prodded at one of the indentations. 'Seem real enough, though.'

They both walked back to the bed and sat on it.

'Doctor Frankenstein said he would stop lying to me from now on, so I should be able to ask if they're real or not and what they have to do with the condition.'

Brian cocked his head to one side. 'And would we believe him?'

'No, of course not. I need to find someone unconnected with the trial to confirm it.'

Dan got up and went to the window. 'It would need to be someone from outside, but we're not allowed to leave the hospital.'

Brian joined him. 'We may not have to. Plenty of visitors must come and go all the time – just ask an electrician or some other tradesman.'

They spotted a figure in the distance and spoke at the same time. 'A gardener!'

Dan's last attempt at trying to get someone to look at part of his body was pointed out. 'Are you going to keep your clothes *on* this time?'

Dan ignored Brian and sat back on the bed. He looked at his minder through the open door. He was wondering how to get past him when Lisa blocked the view.

'Good afternoon, Dan. How are you getting on with the exercises I left you with?'

She cocked her head at the untouched exercise ball and leaflet. Dan peered around her.

'That's okay, Lisa. I'll be, er, leaving the hospital in the next couple of days, so won't be needing physiotherapy anymore.'

She folded her arms. 'Well, that means I won't get paid, which means I won't be able to feed and clothe my children. Do you really want that on your conscience when you, *er*, leave?'

Dan guessed all the staff must know about his suicide risk. He was about to give her short shrift when he noticed something different: she'd had a boob job done. Or, rather, Lisa *looked* as if she'd had a boob job done, but that was impossible as she was flat-chested yesterday. He smirked at what must have been done to create the appearance when she smiled back at him. His jaw dropped. She was now beautiful too. And *younger*, yes – much younger than he had remembered. Wider, rounder, and deeper blue eyes. Fuller and redder lips. A more petite, dainty nose, and curves he was positive didn't exist just twenty-four hours ago.

The skinny, middle-aged woman he'd judged to be a hard-nosed lesbian was now a stunning blonde in her twenties. She looked like something out of *Vogue* magazine. He blinked a couple of times. She was still beautiful. Dan grabbed the exercise ball and squeezed it hard to check he hadn't fallen asleep again. It hurt like blazes.

Lisa saw his pain and reached out to take the ball. Her hands were beautiful too. Not a wrinkle, vein, or tendon in sight – just a smooth, clean, fresh complexion. Even her nails were manicured. Dan was now used to the look of his own hands, but the contrast between her youthful grace and his evil-looking talons was still stark. *What the hell's going on with me*? he thought to himself. He ran a hand over his scalp.

'Lisa?'

Her appearance was so captivating, he had to look away to ask the question.

'What are these marks on my head?'

'They're from your operation. Did you forget you had them?'

'I must have done.'

Brian tossed his head in disgust at how easily Dan gave in to a pretty face. Dan tried shaking himself out of the siren-like grip.

'Can we go into the gardens for some exercise today?'

Lisa thought that was an excellent idea and prepared his wheelchair. Dan couldn't take his eyes off her. It was nothing sexual. No, it was like looking at something important he had lost or was gone forever – like the death of a friend or old flame he still pined for. The feeling was similar to viewing a photograph album and wondering how time could have passed by so quickly and unnoticed.

Dan settled into the wheelchair and tried to put it out of his mind. Lisa pushed him into the corridor. He was reminded of being outside his previous room and coming face to face with the occupant opposite. Only this time he wasn't looking at the disfigured form of a man with the same condition as him, but at a person who could not have been more different if he'd tried.

The orderly stood up to acknowledge Lisa's charge and, straight away, Dan was struck by the man's handsome looks, height, and muscular physique – Dan felt inadequate by comparison. He only saw the orderly for a few seconds, but it was enough to acknowledge the hospital appeared to have gained a second perfect physical specimen in the prime of youth. Dan made two fists to ensure he was still awake.

They had to wait for the lift and Dan's eyes wandered down the corridor to see yet another beauty like Lisa in charge of a similar wheelchair. The occupant looked straight back at him, and Dan just had time to think it was someone he knew when both doors opened and each party continued their respective journeys. Dan promptly forgot about him.

Lisa took Dan down to the ground floor and, after passing further impressive examples of human perfection, Dan realised his mind had found some new way of torturing him during his waking hours. If the indentations on his scalp were real, his next step would be to establish any link.

He studied his hands. They couldn't be more opposite to these new hallucinations – not knowing the true nature of his condition was frustrating. Lisa wheeled him down the corridor that led to the conservatory, and Dan wondered if his fellow patients would be just as imposing.

'That's all I need,' he said to himself. 'Gary looking like a miserable Sean Connery.'

They entered the conservatory and Dan was relieved to see his brain had chosen not to represent them as paragons of youth for some reason, but all the same they were different. He couldn't put his finger on it, but everyone appeared to be 'normal'. Not just in the social conduct of conversation, reading, and the playing of various board games – they looked better too.

The condition they all shared was still apparent but visually acceptable now. Some even seemed to have been cured of it – until Dan drew closer and realised the damage was still plain to see. He scrutinised his hands for a third time in as many minutes. *What is this?*

As Lisa wheeled him out of the conservatory, they passed Gary, who put his head down when he saw the two of them, giving Dan the chance to confirm a third thing they had in common – head scars. Dan was now more determined than ever to confirm their reality. Lisa pushed him onto the patio and he was pleased to see the gardener still working about twenty yards away. She applied the brakes.

'Right, how do you intend to impress me first?'

Dan didn't take his eyes off the groundsman. 'I think I could walk all the way from here to the bottom of the garden and back again without any help whatsoever.'

He turned to smile, but had to look away when the sight of Lisa made him feel just as inadequate as the orderly did. His eyes then caught sight of the barbecue and he recalled the feeling when being made to re-enact his accident with it – a sense of being played for a fool. Only this time it seemed to be Mother Nature enjoying the experience at his expense. He faced the gardener again.

'I'm impressed with your ambition already! Okay, off you go – I'll wait for you here.'

Dan placed both feet on the grass and stood up. It was another glorious day and he turned his face up to bask in it. He dropped his head again when the sun's rays seemed to eat into his skin. The pain stopped, as did a feeling of melting around his face and neck.

'Damn these hallucinations,' he said to himself,

but not before wondering if nature wanted to finish something she started six months ago. Dan concentrated on the man in the distance and walked.

He was soon close enough to see a flowerbed being tended. Various plants and shrubs proliferated, with tall sunflowers dominating the scene. He was just feet from the gardener when Dan heard a thump and one of the sunflowers shook. A petal fell from it. The sun glinted off the blade that was brought down for a second time – the plant then crashed to the ground. The sunflower appeared to be in full bloom and, when the head of another healthy-looking specimen shook, Dan quickened his pace. He made a fist on the way. It still hurt.

'What on earth do you think you're doing? There's nothing wrong with those flowers!'

The second plant was about to tumble too when the gardener stood up.

'I'm afraid they've had their day.'

'What are you talking about? They're beautiful!'

The gardener surveyed the remaining thirteen plants. 'You mean they *were* beautiful.'

Dan scanned them. The sunflowers were tall, with the familiar dinner-plate of seeds, but their stems were starting to bend, leaves drooped and petals lay on the ground. Their heads no longer appeared capable of looking into the sun – just like Dan. The feeling of nature playing him for a fool increased.

'But there *must* be something you can do – it seems so *wrong*.'

The groundsman took off his gloves and placed both them and the knife onto the ground. 'I could, but it wouldn't last for long and they'd never be as beautiful again. I'm afraid nature won't let us keep anything young forever.'

Dan's stomach turned. The gardener pointed out some seedlings.

'Why persist with the old when the young can take their place?'

Dan sank to his knees. Lisa ran to him.

The gardener was concerned. 'Are you all right?'

'I just need to sit here for a while.'

Dan rested a hand on the grass. The individual blades and small wild flowers between reminded him of something. He half expected to see a bumble bee and wasn't disappointed – the flowers in the bed were teeming with them.

The gardener explained the cycle of life. 'Nothing gets wasted.' He gestured towards the slain sunflower. 'The leaves, stems, and head will go to compost and the birds will eat the seeds.'

As the man spoke, a sparrow alighted on the dead plant and did just that. Dan looked, but his brain made sure he saw something very different. The hallucination this time was of a crow pecking at the eyes of a rotting cadaver. Dan closed his own, tight.

Lisa caught up and knelt down. 'Are you okay, Dan?'

'We're all going to die.'

She made light of the comment. 'We certainly are. Along with taxes it's one of life's certainties, I'm afraid.' Dan didn't respond. She put an arm around his shoulders. 'Do you want to go back inside now?'

Dan opened his eyes and pulled himself together. 'Yes – but I'd like to try on my own again.'

He put out a hand and both Lisa and the gardener helped him to his feet. Dan set out in the direction of the conservatory.

Doctor Adams was standing in the entrance to the corridor at the far end of the conservatory when Dan arrived. The grip was tightened on the gardener's knife.

Dan's brain lost no time in ensuring he continued to witness further hallucinations of death and decay. Everyone but the staff appeared to be withering and dying right before his eyes.

He watched in revulsion as Gary put out a hand, only for it decompose and putrefy, until all that was left was a desiccated husk of bones in a shroud of rotted skin. Dan knew it was his brain playing with him, but it was still a sickening sight.

He looked at the rest of the patients who, like the dying sunflowers, were no longer capable of holding their heads up. He tried to ignore the horror of disintegrating hair and flesh falling from their bodies, like the leaves and petals of the ageing plants. Dan knew there was a message for him here somewhere, but didn't care. He just wanted to get to the person responsible for it all.

Dan's hands were becoming used to pain, so he pressed a thumb against the edge of the blade. The threshold of agony reset. Blood ran over the handle at the same time so Dan squeezed it harder to maintain his grip.

Tracy stood next to the doctor. Dan had seen her become slimmer and prettier almost by the hour, yet her beauty still took him aback. She was now even younger, renewed almost back to her teens. For a moment he thought the orderly from outside his room had replaced Adams, but realised he too had undergone a similar transformation; early middle-aged spread, jowls, and greying hair had all gone, to be replaced by a firm, young, and muscular appearance. The comparison between them and the decay of living corpses all around could not have been starker.

That difference made Dan stop. Decay and renewal was the message, but he couldn't think what that had to do with the condition. What was his brain trying to tell him? Something tugged at his elbow and Dan looked down to see Alice presenting him with her doll. It too was in an advanced state of decay and crumbled to dust the moment Dan touched it. Alice's decomposing face pleaded with him to do something and, illusion or not, he implored the doctor to help her but just as before, when Dan couldn't breathe, Adams did nothing.

Like the rest of the patients, Alice's features were putrefying fast – her already thin lips soon melted away into a grotesque smile of rotted teeth. Dan looked at Tracy, only to see her lips become fuller and redder in response. She ran her tongue over her own teeth as if to show off how perfectly pearl-like and uniform they were. She appeared to be revelling in her restored youth at Alice's expense.

Maggots entered and devoured Alice's wide-open eyes and on through the rest of her now exposed skull. Dan turned to Tracy again and to his disgust, her eyes became rounder, fuller, bluer, and even more beautiful in response. Even her hair seemed to parasitically absorb what little life Alice had left in hers.

Dan didn't care that it was all an illusion. He snapped. 'WHAT HAVE YOU DONE TO HER? SHE'S ONLY A LITTLE GIRL!'

Tracy's response was incredulous. She put her head on the doctor's chest and stared adoringly up at him. A physically perfect young man looked lovingly back down. She then took the doctor's hand and placed it on her swelling abdomen. Dan closed his eyes and raised the knife to strike, just as the gardener reached from behind and took it from him.

The condition meant Dan didn't notice, and he continued with the intent, only to place a bloody hand on the doctor's shoulder. The exertion sapped Dan's energy and he had to hold on to recover. The two lovers then looked away and into the corridor behind, where there was movement. They separated as if encouraging Dan to investigate.

A frail old man blocked his way. He was stooped and his limbs and head shook. Saliva drooled profusely from a slack jaw. He stared back at Dan. The old man was by no means in an illusionary state of post-mortem decay like the rest of the patients, but he wasn't far from it.

Dan experienced a strange empathy for him. He put out a hand to try and express it, just as the old man did the same. His hand was covered in blood, too. Dan looked the old man in the eye, but both became distracted by something cold, hard and metal-like between them. They turned to see their hands were flat against each other, and straight away Dan noticed they were identical in every respect – right down to how the blood dripped off each.

Dan stared at his reflection in the mirror. 'BUT I'M A YOUNG MAN!'

Not any more he wasn't. He raised his hands to his face. How could he have got it so wrong? How could he have mistaken the wrinkled and wasted flesh of a decrepit old man for the burns and accident damage of someone in the prime of life? Because of what had been done to his brain. That was how. What they had done to him on the trial. He now understood the meaning of the hallucinations. He now understood the condition. Whatever had been done to him and the other patients had increased their rate of ageing. They were all dying of old age – half a century too soon.

Dan wanted more than ever for the torture to end. He had to die. He *must* die, but then it struck him. The orderly, Lisa, Tracy, Adams, and all the rest.

He recalled Tony's words: 'There's always some new medical advance to make you live longer.'

It seemed fantastically impossible, which was why his brain had to exaggerate their appearance to ensure he understood – the hospital's staff were part of the trial too.

He couldn't even begin to understand how it was happening, but, like increasingly beautiful parasites, they were sucking the life out of him and the others – just so theirs could be restored and extended. The gardener was wrong. A way to perpetuate flowers had been found, but at a terrible cost – accelerated decrepitude for those less deserving. Like front-line soldiers sacrificed in battle, he and all the other patients had served their purpose and could now be discarded.

Dan became angry. Who were they to decide who should live and who should die? What gave them the right? It was an abomination against nature which Dan had to expose in whatever time he had left. He looked back at himself in the mirror and wondered how long that was. With each passing second, the human leeches seem to drain more and more life from him. The little hair he had left on his head appeared to be falling out and he reached up to touch it. More came away. He ran a finger down one cheek. It split. Dan panicked.

'NO! NOT YET!' He put his bloodied hand up to smear the image from view, as if being out of sight would put a stop to it, but that just presented a limb that had begun to mummify. 'NO! NO!'

In desperation he turned to Doctor Adams just as a drop of blood appeared to hang in front of Dan's face. His eyesight was deteriorating fast, but he knew what it was. His legs buckled. He had no choice – Dan lunged at the red pill.

PART TWO

CHAPTER ONE

'So, how's the fountain of youth coming along?'

Professor Savage glanced around the club. As a member of parliament, Alex Salib had impressed her superiors enough to be considered a rising star, but any more off-hand comments like that and she would be lucky to serve the rest of her time on the back benches, let alone as a future prime minister.

A couple of the broadsheets rustled disapprovingly, but more out of annoyance at the disruption to the genteel atmosphere than the damage a breach of confidence might cause. The professor leaned forward and lowered his voice.

'If you must refer to the discovery as some kind of elixir, then I'm afraid it's more one of health rather than youth.' He sat back in the armchair. 'I'm sorry if that disappoints you.'

Alex looked at her surroundings. She despised old-guard establishments at the best of times, and a gentlemen's club that had only recently allowed women in as guests, let alone members, was about as far removed from her politics as it was possible to get. Throw in a hoary old professor of medicine with blood on his hands via animal vivisection, and it could be argued that the only reason she became a member of parliament in the first place was to ensure their retirement.

Still, she'd only recently won her seat and, if being a member of a cross-party health committee meant having to appear more centrist for a while, then so be it. They were a dying breed anyway and, like any species heading for extinction, she felt sorry for them so decided to abide by their petty rules – for now.

She leaned forward in her seat and adopted a tone she hoped didn't patronise too much. 'Well, if you wish to secure more funding, then I'm afraid it's going to have to be some kind of miracle cure at the very least.' She sat back again. 'I'm sorry if that disappoints you.'

The professor sighed inside. It was all so easy a couple of generations ago. One was born a gentleman destined for high office, one grew up with other gentlemen equally set for great things. One went to Eton or Harrow, then Oxbridge with them; went to war with them; shit, showered, shaved, and even shagged with one or two of them; and if you were still close after all that, then the vulgar subject of money was never even discussed, let alone begged for.

He studied her. He'd seen the country's newest MP at a distance, but this was their first meeting and certainly the first time he knew his fabled charm would be of little use. It wasn't just the fact that she was a self-proclaimed lesbian transgender (whatever that was), but mainly because she was about as far removed from him as it was possible to be.

Born on a kitchen-sink estate to a single white mother and absentee refugee father from a war-torn Middle Eastern country, her modest education consisted of comprehensive school, a first in law at some polytechnic masquerading as a university, and then straight into politics to help save the planet. Everything a darling of the left should be. She even used a wheelchair for goodness' sake. If ever there was a politician engendered to secure the sympathy vote, she was it. Indeed, if it wasn't for her disabilities, one could imagine her a prize specimen, plucked straight from the old left's great melting pot of humanity.

He speculated on her condition. Like most medical men, he'd always at least subconsciously diagnosed a visible ailment upon first sight, together with the social group suggested. He knew it was judgemental, but that was just the way he was. It was nothing personal.

Her posture and pallor indicated a number of complex conditions and he estimated she would probably succumb to at least one of them within the next ten years. Plenty of time to achieve her political ambitions, but still sad nonetheless. She was dying and, like any species heading for extinction, he felt sorry for her, so decided to abide by her petty rules – for now.

He adopted a tone he hoped didn't patronise too much. 'What if I were to tell you it has the potential to cure many disabilities?'

Alex corrected him. 'You mean "impairments".'

Savage sat back in his chair again and tried not to be irritated by the lesson in political correctness.

She didn't labour the point.

'What's the catch?'

Savage made his pitch. 'The catch is, money is needed to extend the trial so the efficacy of the discovery can be tested on other equally deserving sections of society.'

The truth was, Alex had already been briefed on the importance of the professor's work and instructed to give him whatever he wanted but a determined personal ambition meant she was keen to exercise independence of thought too.

'Not if the research involves animals, abuse of the unborn or any other creature unable to make its own decision.'

It felt good to get on to a subject she was passionate about. The professor became quiet for a moment.

'Ms Salib, have you any idea of the impact a discovery like this could have on the lives of millions of ordinary people? Not to mention the literally billions of pounds of savings to the National Health Service and social care budgets. And what do you think your *fountain of youth* could be worth to the exchequer in terms of foreign drug sales?'

Alex didn't answer. She didn't give a damn. She knew she had to do her colleagues' bidding, but if helping people came at the expense of innocents, she was vehemently against it – regardless of how many it helped and especially if money was to be made from suffering.

The professor glanced around the anteroom before leaning towards her and lowering his voice again. 'Now, if that means I get to sadistically enjoy inserting red-hot needles into the eyes of bunny rabbits and babies so you and millions of others can regain the simple pleasure of walking again, then I trust you would be willing to compromise on your admirable, if somewhat naïve, principles?'

CHAPTER TWO

'Come on, Danny – wake up!'

'Wake up, Dad.' It was his daughter's voice.

Someone took hold of his left hand. For a second, he thought both his wife and daughter must be with him.

'Dad, can you hear me?'

His hand was being caressed. He opened his eyes. Not in the conservatory any more.

'Dad, do you recognise me?'

He squinted at the shock of blonde hair. It never ceased to amaze him how much Lucy looked like her mother. Or was it the other way around? Claire didn't seem to be with her.

'Where's your mother?' he croaked.

Lucy didn't answer. He focussed on her and tried to smile.

'Boy, are you a sight for sore eyes. Where am I?'

He scanned the room and saw the hoist, the window back in its usual place, and that damn clock still annoyingly stuck at the same time. Dan answered his own question. 'Back in my old room. How did I get here?'

'Try not to stress yourself, you're still very weak.'

Dan lifted his right arm and, as expected, his hand

was bandaged. He winced at the memory of slicing his fingers into the blade to ensure the horrors were just hallucinations. A glance at his left hand confirmed they were no longer being manifested. It still hurt to move his fingers, though. He recalled the illusion of his face decaying.

'I need a mirror.'

Lucy rummaged through her handbag, opened a compact, and passed it to him. Dan raised it to his eyes.

Despite knowing it couldn't possibly have been real, he still expected the worst, but, to his surprise, his face was back to normal – just as Tony said it would be. The red pill had worked. He recalled Doctor Adams' words: 'Unless you resume your medication, you're highly likely to experience the worst horrors the mind can produce.' An understatement if ever there was one.

Dan sighed with the relief. The nightmare was over. Lucy had her head down – her lower lip protruded slightly. He reached forward, pushed it back in and tickled her under the chin. Both their faces lit up with smiles and yet more tears as they embraced. Father and daughter reunited at last.

There was a knock and Adams entered. He smiled at Lucy, which annoyed Dan just as much as when he smiled at Claire. There may have been nothing sinister about the red pill after all, but Dan still didn't trust him.

'Awake, I see. Good morning – do you know who I am?'

Dan wiped his eyes before replying: 'Doctor Adams.'

The doctor uttered some more pleasantries before

taking his patient's temperature and pulse, and then checking over the bandages. It gave Dan a chance to confirm the young, muscular Adonis had returned to normal too. Back to mid-forties, he guessed. Tall with dark hair greying at the sides. Dan still couldn't warm to him but there was one difference – Dan didn't feel sorry for himself. He guessed the illusions of exaggerated youth and beauty were just his mind's way of getting him to acknowledge what the red pill had now made obvious.

'I'm afraid these dressings will be needed for a while. Mind if I ask you a few questions?'

'Sure.' Dan was looking forward to answering them this time.

'What's your name?'

Dan looked at his daughter. 'I'd like to say Winston Churchill, but no one seems to appreciate my sense of humour, so I guess I'll just have to reply: Squadron Leader Daniel Stewart.'

Lucy turned to the doctor who remained just as expressionless. Dan assumed irony was over their heads too.

'What year is it?'

Dan knew the answer but it felt strange to say. He looked around the room for confirmation, but there was only the annoying digital clock. He checked to see if it also displayed the date, but his vision blurred as he moved closer.

Lucy offered him his glasses and he put them on. The four digits refocussed, as did the twelve months of the year next to them. He now knew why the figures hadn't moved for the last three days – because they weren't meant to. Dan turned away from what had always been a calendar and answered, '2026.'

Lucy jumped up and down in her seat and squeezed his hand. She apologised when he grimaced.

'And how old are you?'

Dan knew the answer to that too but, again, it felt strange to say. So that was the reason for all the subterfuge and lies. That was the reason he had to restart the medication and why the red pill had to be given time to work. Because without it, the truth would have been too horrific to contemplate. He looked at the middle-aged woman holding his normal-looking but arthritic left hand.

He smiled at his daughter then replied: 'Ninety-six.'

The next two questions were answered as expected of a nonagenarian firmly rooted in the twenty-first century, although Dan struggled with them both. Not because he couldn't remember, but because Lucy and he were finding it difficult to contain their excitement. The miracle they were all hoping and praying for had actually happened – Dan's Alzheimer's disease was cured.

Their shouts of joy attracted attention from outside and Tracy, Tony, and others entered, only for the room to then erupt into emotional scenes of congratulatory celebration. That put paid to the doctor's remaining questions, and he was forced to stand back and spectate while the outpourings of joy proceeded.

Dan grinned at him through the throng. The doctor

looked down at his pad and blinked at it a couple of times.

Human after all, thought Dan. The psychologist would have to do more than tremble a bottom lip for his patient to fully trust him.

The melee settled and some of the visitors drifted away to leave close family, Tracy, and Doctor Adams. Dan looked at his saviours and recalled the hallucination of them in the conservatory. He wondered if they were having a relationship in real life, too. They didn't seem suited now they were physically back to normal and the distance they chose to stand apart neither suggested one nor the other. Dan decided the illusion of the two as young lovers expecting a baby amongst all the death and decay was just his brain's way of exaggerating what had happened to him – new life spawning within his brain.

His doctor proceeded by asking some new questions. 'You're holding someone's hand. Can you tell me who that person is?'

For a moment, Dan thought the answer couldn't have been more evident, but played along.

'And who's sitting next to her?'

Again, Dan thought it a strange thing to ask but understood the reason. 'It's her husband – Tony.'

Tony and his wife smiled at each other and held hands. Dan recalled the two of them kissing in the car park and promptly became embarrassed about his loss of control afterwards. He offered to pay for the damage.

'It doesn't matter.'

Adams brought Dan back to what did. 'Does an accident involving an aircraft mean anything to you?'

Dan was about to reiterate his thoughts of it being a figment of his imagination when he realised part of him still felt very much the thirty-six-year-old RAF fighter pilot, living in 1966. He looked at his left hand to confirm his real age, his daughter, her equally middle-aged husband, and the immediate surroundings.

It didn't satisfy, so he got out of bed and went to the window. The hospital had been constructed in the nineteenth century, so only the cars below could be used to confirm it was the twenty-first now. Tony had yet to return the E-type and it stood out as very much the museum piece amongst them all. If Dan was still being lied to, then they'd gone to extraordinary lengths to make him *think* the year was 2026. He turned to Adams.

'Why does part of me still think it's 1966?'

The doctor made a note of that. 'Alzheimer's, I'm afraid. It's robbed you of many long-term memories. If the brain can't reference those any more, then another period can be confused with the present day. In your case, that would appear to be when you were thirty-six. Some sufferers regress all the way back to childhood.'

Dan thought about his fellow patients, and one in particular. 'Like Alice, you mean?'

They all nodded. Dan had been convinced she was a little girl, horribly burnt in the same aircraft accident as him.

'How old is she really?'

Tracy enthused. 'One hundred and eleven next month – she'll be getting another birthday card from the Queen.'

Dan now knew why Alice's mother was dead – she couldn't possibly still be alive. Adams repeated the question about the crash, but Dan couldn't remember anything. He asked a question of his own.

'I take it there actually was an aircraft crash?'

'I need you to answer some other questions first.' The doctor hesitated. 'How would you describe your state of mind at the moment?'

Dan knew what he was alluding to. 'You mean, am I still planning to take my own life?'

The doctor didn't answer. Others in the room shifted with discomfort. Dan took his daughter's hand again.

'Of course not. I couldn't be happier. Whatever you guys have done is simply remarkable – a second shot at life. Not something I could imagine anyone wanting to deliberately squander.'

The sighs of relief were audible. The next question was voiced just as sensitively.

'What can you tell me about your wife?'

It reminded Dan of how much his daughter looked like her. He smiled again, but Lucy didn't smile back this time. Her hair took him back many years to the day he first realised Claire was the one.

They were both fourteen years old and preparing to stage the school pantomime: *Cinderella*. She had the lead, but Dan was just a stagehand. It was a dress rehearsal and one of the teachers had insisted on getting Claire's hair right for the part. School rules meant long hair had to be tied back or plaited, so this was the first time he'd seen her flowing locks. He'd always had a thing for Claire, but the sight of it framing her beauty tipped him into falling in love there and then and, once he'd plucked up the courage to ask her out, she was fool enough to do the same, and the rest, as they say, is history. He chuckled at the row it caused their parents when a week later Claire and he announced their unofficial engagement. He could still see her father ranting and raving while Dan's dad couldn't see what the problem was at all.

Dan stared out of the window. It was another beautiful summer's day, just as it had been then. 'She's dead, isn't she?'

Lucy started to cry. Dan cupped her face. He hoped her almost identical looks would help him to remember his later years with Claire, but they didn't. The earlier joy was replaced by sadness. Lucy put her hand over his. Dan could see it was difficult for her to talk.

'She died of a heart attack five years ago, Dad – around the time you first needed looking after.'

It was like being told for the first time, when in reality Dan must have known for years. He tried to get his head around the shock, but couldn't. The doctor asked another question, but it then occurred to Dan that it wasn't just his wife's death he couldn't remember. *All* of his memories between 1966 and just three days ago seemed to have gone. He tried hard to recall something, anything, from the period, but it was a complete blank. He raised it.

Adams explained Dan's situation, his condition, why he was taking part in the trial, and the stage he was at six months ago on first arriving at the hospital. Alzheimer's disease had robbed him of not only memory, but just about every ability and sense most people take for granted. The pattern of loss had been classic in the years leading up to it. From initial absent-mindedness and repeated episodes of forgetfulness, to an inability to reason, judge, or make simple decisions and perform tasks; this was followed by frustration, irritability, and anger, to personality changes, delusions and, finally, the impairment of basic motor skills needed for physical requirements like dressing, walking, and eating.

By the time Dan had been admitted he'd even forgotten what hunger was, let alone how to open his mouth or swallow food. He was just weeks away from either starving to death or falling victim to a cold most people would simply shrug off. For those who believed in such things, his condition now would indeed seem to be a miracle sent from above.

Adams explained that Dan was just one of sixty million people worldwide with dementia. In that context, his refusal to take the red pill could be seen as an affront to those less fortunate. Dan was ashamed at this apparent ungratefulness, but his doctor made it clear that the ability to exercise emotions again was infinitely more significant than the purpose of them. Even Dan's wish to take his own life had been a demonstration of that – providing he had actually come to terms with it, that is.

It was clear to all that Dan was now in the process of regaining the skills needed to lead a normal life, but what of the missing sixty years? He knew the two people next to his bed were his daughter and her husband, but he couldn't recall anything else about them beyond three days ago. The only other memories of Lucy were when she was a six-year-old. He asked the doctor about that.

'Do you recall your analogy of the brain being like a filing system, albeit a disorganised one?'

Dan nodded.

'Then you'll also remember how a temporary loss of memory could be likened to individual letters falling onto the floor, which the mind can pick up again. But if the floor has holes in it, they can be lost forever. Alzheimer's disease appears to cause holes so large, entire cabinets of files can fall through.'

Dan recalled his dream and the snow of letters pouring like sand over him and the others while he clung on to the crumbling rim.

The doctor continued. 'Even though the treatment is designed to plug those holes and provide new cabinets, the pages in the files are blank and have to be filled in again.'

Dan was puzzled. 'Then how come I've remembered how to walk, eat, and generally take care of myself? I haven't had to relearn it.'

The doctor hesitated before answering. Dan had no problem recalling what that usually meant. What was Adams up to now? Dan knew it was wise to remain wary of him.

'The mystery that is the mind, I'm afraid. You still have months of recovery ahead of you and you may find some of your long-term memory returning, but not as readily as the basics needed for you to lead an independent life again. And, without wishing to pay lip service to your concerns, which would you rather have?'

The doctor asked a question as if to illustrate that. 'Can you remember what you were doing on the twelfth of March 1998?'

Dan thought hard; it must have been something significant for a specific date to be mentioned but he ended up shrugging. The doctor put his notepad away.

'Neither can I, and I suspect nobody else on this planet could recall what they were doing that day either.'

Dan took the point. He tried thinking of something, anything, experienced more than a few days ago, but there was only his accident with the barbecue. He thought of how being made to relive it had recovered the memory, and wondered if something similar could be done to get back the rest of the half century. He looked at Lucy's compact lying open on his bed and realised something had – and successfully, too.

'You deliberately blocked the corridor with that mirror, didn't you?'

Adams glanced at Tracy. 'Not just the corridor – I had a team of people follow you around the hospital with it. Viewing your own reflection was the obvious way to get you to see reality, but each time you did that in your room, your brain knew who it was, so reflected back what it wanted you to see. Placing a mirror in an unusual location freed it of that expectation, allowing your true condition to be revealed – a ninety-six-year-old man recovering from Alzheimer's.'

Dan studied himself in Lucy's compact and, once

again, couldn't decide whether to be impressed or scared at the way the doctor's mind worked.

Dan didn't have any other questions, so the two medical professionals headed for the door. Dan's new short-term memory decided to exercise itself.

'You didn't say if the crash was real or not.'

Adams held the door open for Tracy to leave. '1966 is a long time ago now – the details will need to be researched and we're not keen on allocating resources to something that might not have happened.' He looked at Lucy. 'Google's your best bet.'

He left, and Dan turned excitedly to his daughter. 'Who's Google? Is she a friend of yours?'

Adams addressed Tracy once they were in the corridor. 'Nurse Roberts, I'd like you to prepare my office for a meeting, please.' He looked at his watch. 'In ten minutes, if that's acceptable?'

Tracy checked her own watch and ran what would need to be done through her head. 'Yes, Doctor. That won't be a problem.'

He left her standing there. The doctor was renowned for being emotionally detached, but by addressing her formally she knew how serious the subject would be, and the urgent nature of it. It made her nervous. Still, his office was only two minutes' walk away, so there was plenty of time. Tracy made for the staff restroom.

A short while later she was standing in the office preparing for his arrival as instructed. Doctor Adams often required a meeting straight after a patient had made significant progress, and this occasion would be no different. The room doubled as his call-out accommodation, so Tracy sorted the bed settee first, before turning to the desk.

There were some papers, pens, and other loose stationery items, which she tidied away at one end. Two chairs were moved to better positions. Satisfied with the surroundings, Tracy checked her own appearance. That had already been done once in the restroom, but she looked over herself again to ensure all was still present and correct – the doctor's standards were high and he expected no less of others.

She looked down at her shoes – clean and polished. Stockings – straight, with no snags or ladders. Uniform – a little tight, but otherwise clean and pressed. Apron – unmarked, starched, with fob watch and name badge correctly positioned. Hair – tied up in a tight bun, nothing loose. Hat – spotlessly white, with the correct number of clips holding it in place. She heard footsteps approaching.

The end of the desk faced the entrance and she took up her usual position there with her back to the door. Reaching down to her knees, she grasped the hem of her uniform and pulled it up and over her hips. Her underwear had been removed in the restroom, so Tracy just needed to bend at the waist and lay her chest on the desk for the preparations to be complete. Doctor Adams entered the office and, after adjusting his own clothing, began the meeting as she expected.

CHAPTER THREE

'Are you trying to tell me everyone today not only has a portable television, but it can be used as an encyclopaedia, a typewriter, *and* a telephone?'

Lucy and her husband both laughed.

'And a camera!' Tony added.

Lucy chimed in. 'Don't forget the computer!'

Dan looked at them in disbelief. 'I've seen one of those and they're the size of a room – bigger than the complete set of *Encyclopaedia Britannica* your mother and I bought when you were born. Cost me nearly six months' wages by the time I finished paying for it.'

Lucy made a calculation. 'Well, you can get all that now for less than it costs to feed yourself each day, and in something that will fit into the palm of your hand.'

'Must weigh a ton. You'll be telling me it can read people's minds next.'

'Only a matter of time,' said Tony.

He passed Dan his iPhone. Dan took hold of it like one would a photograph, and the screen image moved under his thumb. He screwed his face up and gave it straight back.

Lucy and Tony stopped laughing as the size of the

task that lay ahead dawned on them. Moon landings, the first female British prime minister, the internet, the first black American president, self-driving cars – these and much more would have to be either recalled or learned from scratch all over again. At least the threat to humanity by global nuclear annihilation seemed to have subsided a bit since 1966.

Lucy took her father's hand. 'Dad, you've no idea how good it feels to have you back – even if you have forgotten everything about me from when I was six to just three days ago.'

Her father looked at her lovingly, just as he had done for decades. They both knew that was what really mattered.

'When was the last time you saw Brian, Dan?'

Father and daughter looked at Tony.

Dan shrugged. 'He's probably been to see me at some stage – I guess I've forgotten that too. Mind you, he's a couple of years older than me, so I suppose he could even be dead by now.' His eyes flitted between the two of them. 'Is he?'

The couple looked at each other before Tony spoke again.

'No, what I meant was: have you had any more hallucinations of him?'

Dan appeared to conduct a visual search of the room.

'No, although he, er, I mean *it*, generally only appears when I'm on my own. Maybe he's gone for good now I'm taking the red pill again.' He picked up Lucy's compact and prodded one of the dents in his skull. 'So what's been done to me exactly?' Lucy looked at her husband to provide the answer.

'Stem-cell therapy. New brain cells are cultivated and then planted where they're needed in your skull. The red pill and you thinking nice thoughts does the rest.'

Dan looked at Tony as if he was the one who needed brain surgery. 'Stem what?'

Lucy and Tony realised there was something else that would need explaining all over again.

There was a knock on the door and a nurse entered. The small translucent tub in her hand told them all it was pill time again. Husband and wife took that as their cue to leave. Lucy asked her father if there was anything he needed, but nothing occurred to him. She made a suggestion.

'Something to throw through a window, perhaps?'

Dan stuck his tongue out. 'I always knew you had my sense of humour!'

They left and the nurse offered Dan the tub and a beaker of water. A red pill was nestling amongst two other, paler ones. He got out of bed, took them from her, and walked over to the window. He soon saw Lucy and Tony making their way hand in hand towards the car park.

He watched as they stopped at the entrance and turn to face each other. Dan picked up the red pill and placed it on his tongue. He raised the cup to his lips and smiled when he saw Tony raise Lucy's lips to his.

CHAPTER FOUR

Tracy put her head on his chest and he pulled the covers up over them both.

'Will he live?'

'Who?'

'Your patient, of course. The reason why you wanted to have sex.'

Adams kissed the top of her head. 'I'm sure I don't know what you mean.'

She playfully pinched him. 'Don't give me that. I've known you for over twenty years – I know exactly how your mind works.'

The doctor reflected on their time together. 'I hardly think reading you bedtime stories when you were eight counts as the start of our relationship.'

Tracy insisted. 'Don't let the facts get in the way. We may only have met again three years ago, but that was when I first fell in love with you, which is what counts.'

The doctor tried to get his head around the concept. Not of eight-year-old girls falling in love with twenty-four-year-old babysitters going out with their nineteen-year-old cousins, but of love itself. He'd experienced it, of course, not least with Tracy's cousin, but what seemed to happen so naturally back then appeared to require more of an effort now.

Which was strange, as Tracy was almost exactly like her cousin and certainly the reason why he had initiated the relationship in the first place – he wanted to recapture the love of his life. She wasn't her, of course, but, perhaps just as importantly, nor was he a young, soon-to-be-qualified doctor any more. He cared for Tracy and would do anything for her – but love? It was such an alien concept these days.

Adams answered her question. 'He still has a long way to go and the treatment only replaces the cells damaged by dementia. It doesn't cure the underlying cause, so surgery will be required again at some stage.' He thought of the most likely outcome. 'Alzheimer's aside, he still has other conditions to contend with. Angina, Parkinson's, emphysema – you name it. He's much more likely to succumb to one of those first.'

Tracy snuggled up. 'I'm still proud of you, though.'

Adams played down his part in Dan's progress. 'It's Professor Savage you should be impressed with – he's the genius behind the science. I'm just a whipping boy needed to conduct his trial, although I do question why he selected such physically weak candidates. Seems a waste to spend so much time and effort on patients who could all drop dead at any sec—' He broke off when he realised Tracy was giving him some kind of physical examination – her fingers probed his abdomen. 'What are you doing?'

'Just checking out my investments.'

'And?'

'Not bad – for your age.'

He poked out his tongue. She grinned and pulled herself closer.

'It's such a shame. Giving someone a second chance at life is an incredible achievement – you only had to look at the emotion in his daughter's face to see that.' Tracy looked up at him. 'Or the emotion in yours.' They kissed. 'I love it when Mr Grumpy's true feelings come out.'

Adams jokingly denied the existence of them. 'My dear young lady, do I look like the kind of person to suffer such basic human weaknesses?'

He tickled her. Tracy grabbed his manhood.

'My dear sir, do I look like the kind of person to suffer such basic human bullshit?'

She let go as a half-serious look of panic appeared on his face. He relaxed. She giggled.

'What are you laughing at now?'

'You and your silly rituals.'

Adams kept up the fake denials. 'What rituals? I could tell you wanted sex and merely suggested one of our regular meetings.'

She pinched him. 'We both know full well which one of us initiated it and why – you don't need to be a psychologist to work it out.'

The doctor pleaded ignorance. 'That comes under psychosexuality, which I never studied, I'm afraid – you'd need to speak to a specialist.'

Tracy propped herself up on an elbow. 'I don't need

to – every woman's one when it comes to understanding men and their strange needs.'

'Okay, Doctor Richards, give me your diagnosis.'

Tracy took up the challenge and pondered his sexual proclivities. 'Well, by your own admission, even after our fun, you still masturbate at least five to ten times a day and view internet pornography whenever you can, which means you have a high sex drive. Couple the prolific nature of that with a life governed by a strict series of moral disciplinary codes, and is it any wonder those two worlds collide to create some kind of sexual OCD when faced with an emotion you can't immediately control?'

He was genuinely impressed. Adams referred to himself in the third person. 'Sounds like the poor chap's a hopeless case. Is there a treatment?'

Tracy put her head back on his chest. 'I can heartily recommend a dose of marriage, followed by a course of children.' She looked back up. 'Under my personal and very close supervision.'

He made out to consider her proposal. 'And the prognosis?'

Tracy kissed him on the lips. 'A very happy ever after for us all.'

'Hmmm. I shall give your professional opinion careful consideration and get back to you as soon as I can. In the meantime, fancy a quick one?'

Tracy got off the bed settee and began to get dressed. Her change in mood was palpable. 'Darling, what's the matter?'

She rolled up a stocking and slipped her toes into it.

'You know exactly what the matter is. Every time I get serious about us, you respond with humour.'

He put a hand on her shoulder but it was shrugged off. Tracy stood up. 'It's the same old story. You get what you want, when you want it, and sod my feelings and needs.'

Adams tried, but just couldn't bring himself to say what he knew she wanted to hear. 'Darling, it's not like that – you know how much I care about you.'

Tracy stopped. 'Care? Don't you mean something else? You "care" for patients or the elderly – you're meant to feel something completely different towards someone you seriously intend spending the rest of your life with.'

He didn't respond. She persisted.

'Go on then. Say it. You know what I want to hear.'

The doctor avoided her gaze and looked down at the floor in silence. She shook her head, finished dressing, and walked over to the door.

'Do you know what? I feel sorry for you and do you want to know why? Because with all the incredible things being done in this hospital, you could be anything you want, but without a wife and family to love and be loved by, you'll just end up a sad old man, dying alone.'

Adams pictured the scene. *That's going to happen to us all anyway*, he thought to himself.

Tracy employed a more sympathetic but just as steadfast tone. 'Darling, I'm pushing thirty and you're the wrong side of forty – if this relationship is going to mean anything, then it has to move to the next stage.' Her eyes welled. 'If you don't want that, then I'm sorry, but I'm going to have to find someone who does.' She unlocked the door and left.

The doctor's office seemed emptier than her leaving would have suggested and he became despondent. Tracy was right, of course. At the very least, all living species were supposed to replace themselves at some stage, but he knew he could no more spend the rest of his life with the same woman than practise in the same hospital or drive the same car.

Maybe there was something wrong with him? Millions of other men seemed to manage monogamy okay. The trouble was, millions of married men also cheated on their wives and, as silly as 'a life governed by a strict series of moral disciplinary codes' sounded, it wouldn't let him do that. The result? A succession of monogamous relationships that never went anywhere.

He wasn't worried about her leaving him. He was always the one who both ended and initiated his relationships and in the same way – when a new opportunity or model came along. He knew it seemed shallow and heartless, but he couldn't help the way he was.

It couldn't go on forever, of course – it was only a matter of time before women started doing the same to him, so something had to give. Adams thought fondly of Tracy. She really would make an ideal wife and mother. If a potion existed to make him fall in love with her as much as she was with him, he would take it.

CHAPTER FIVE

'Ah! The prodigal son returns!'

After his refusal to take the red pill, Dan thought he probably deserved Gary's greeting. Tracy parked the wheelchair opposite him in silence, which was unusual for her. She'd seemed preoccupied with something on their way to the conservatory, but Dan thought it best not to pry. Her walk away was just as stilted. He called her back.

'Tracy? Any chance of a cup of tea?'

Her reply made him question if it would be safe to drink.

'Of course, Dan. Anything you want, Dan. After all, isn't that what we women are for? To give men what they want, just for the pleasure of having served them?' She walked away.

Gary became confused. 'What was that all about?'

Dan was just as perplexed. 'Beats me. Time of the month?'

'Nah, there'll be a man involved somewhere. Anyway, glad to see you took my advice at last. How does it feel to be back in the land of the living?'

Dan looked around the conservatory at his fellow

inmates, who still appeared to be about his age – just not the one he thought he was. 'I suppose it depends on what you mean by "living". We're all stuck in a hospital at the moment.'

Gary smiled, which didn't look right to Dan – being miserable suited him better. 'Yeah, but not for long. Not once Professor Savage has finished performing his magic.'

'Who's Professor Savage?'

Gary gave a look as if Dan had been born yesterday, which in many respects, he had. 'Only the person who's saved your life, that's all.'

Dan glanced at the other patients again. 'Is a ninety-six-year-old's life worth saving?'

Gary remained upbeat. 'Of course it is.' He leaned towards Dan. 'You're a mere boy – most of us here are centenarians.' He pointed. 'Alice will be a hundred and eleven soon.'

She smiled and waved. Dan grinned and nodded back. He guessed whatever this Professor Savage did for a living had worked on her too. The doll was nowhere to be seen, so he assumed that, like him, she was also now aware of her actual age. She looked every minute of it, though. Dan grimaced at the recollection of her face decaying. He still couldn't get over how he'd mistaken her for a little girl, horribly burnt by fire.

'How old are you, then?'

Gary's smile turned to a toothy grin, which suited him even less. 'One-hundred and five!' he said proudly.

Dan thought he looked every second of that too, but

was amazed at how positive he was with the idea – like a whole different person. Dan regarded the scars on Gary's head. 'So, does the professor's magic cure depression as well as amnesia? Up until yesterday, I thought of nothing but suicide.'

Gary became serious. 'That's because you stopped taking the red pill.' He sat back in his chair. 'The treatment does a lot more than cure dementia – it opens your eyes.'

Dan was about to ask what he meant by that when Tracy arrived back with the tea. Some of it spilt as the cups were slapped down onto the table. She made a swift exit before either of them could say anything. Dan scraped his cup against its saucer and took a sip. He sucked his teeth and put it back into the puddle.

'What do you mean by "opens your eyes"?'

Gary checked to see who else might be listening, and for a second Dan thought he was going to tell him to mind his own business again, but he didn't. He did lean forward, though.

'Let's just say that whatever you thought was right about yourself before will turn out to be completely wrong.' The annoying smile reappeared.

Dan sighed. 'Well, that's obvious. Up until yesterday, I thought I was a thirty-six-year-old pilot in the RAF, but now it's as plain as day I'm a ninety-six-year-old retired one.'

'You don't understand. That's just your history. I'm talking about the *way* you used to think.'

Dan tried to understand what he was getting at. He looked at Tracy.

'Well, I lusted after a certain nurse a few days ago, but that's because I thought I was a red-blooded young man back in 1966 and those breasts of hers would definitely have appealed back then. Now I've been brought back kicking and screaming into the twenty-first century, my thoughts towards her have changed completely – more paternal now. In fact, if it is a man who's upset her, I'd like to meet him so I can punch him on the nose, like any caring father would.'

'No, you wouldn't.' Gary seemed to think he knew him better. 'The red pill or, rather, the surgery and drugs, won't let you. You don't know it yet, but it will come. Your mind has been altered in more ways than one and all for the better – you're much more relaxed about things now.'

Dan could see he wasn't the only one whose treatment had yet to be completed. 'It's just the soporific nature of the drugs, Gary. Once the trial is over, you'll stop being so damn positive about things and be back to your same old miserable self.' Dan smiled for a change. 'Which will make us both very happy.'

'Okay then, let's talk about the politics of social class.'

Dan sighed again and tried to catch Tracy's eye.

'You and I are poles apart when it comes to that and the old me had a huge chip on his shoulder about it, but not now – I honestly couldn't give a damn.'

She spotted Dan and he motioned for her to extract him from Gary's ramblings as soon as possible. Whatever drugs he was on were either kicking in or wearing off, and Dan didn't want to be around to find out which. Tracy made her way over while Gary went on.

'It's amazing; I can't believe how much I used to detest everything about you and your kind. I firmly believed the entire corrupt and self-serving system needed bringing down, and the sooner you were all put up against a wall and shot, the better.'

Tracy released the brakes on Dan's wheelchair. Gary grabbed his arm. 'If someone had told me a week ago that I would not only know my place but be perfectly happy to be in it, I would have killed them.' He let go, flopped back in his chair, and sobbed. 'You've no idea how happy I am now.'

Tracy pulled Dan away just as Gary appeared to cry himself to sleep.

'Is that going to happen to me?' Dan was beginning to think there were side-effects to the treatment that had yet to be explained.

Whatever preoccupied Tracy was still there. 'What do you mean *going to*? Seriously planning to take your own life for the past couple of days is rational behaviour, I suppose?'

Dan took the point, but the change in Gary still bothered him. 'I know, but that was because I wasn't taking my medication but I am now. Will I soon be rambling like a madman too?'

Tracy became more professional. 'Dan. At the risk of repeating myself, you're taking part in a clinical trial. Trials produce both expected and unexpected results, and it's my duty to report on both. If I see something in your behaviour which fits either description or you wish me to pass something on to he who must be obeyed, then that's exactly what I'll do.'

How Tracy referred to Adams didn't go unnoticed. Dan narrowed his view of her and she responded by moving behind the wheelchair to avoid it. She began pushing him back to his room.

The return journey was as quiet as the one out, but this time Dan knew why. He still thought it best not to be nosey, though – until they got back to his room and he saw how sad she looked. He wanted to hug her like a granddaughter, but didn't think it appropriate. He thought it wise not to mention Doctor Adams by name either.

'The bastard's not worth it, Tracy – you can do much better.' He clenched his fists, which hurt him of course. 'I knew there was a good reason why I've never liked him.'

Tracy sat down and let the tears go. Dan decided to put his arm around her after all.

'There, there. It's okay – shhh. A beautiful young girl like you – someone much more deserving is bound to come along soon.'

Tracy seemed to appreciate the concern more than the solution. 'What is it about men, Dan? Why can't they see something that's so obvious to us women?'

Dan thought about the day he first fell in love with Claire. 'I'm afraid you're asking the wrong person, Tracy.' He recounted how he met and eventually married his Cinderella. It made Tracy cry all the more.

'That's so romantic. Seventy-seven years together – you must really miss her.'

He certainly did, and more than Dan was prepared to admit. The significance of waking up and realising he could only remember the first twenty-two years of their life was just beginning to register.

He turned his attention back to Tracy. 'There are plenty of good men out there – you just have to be patient.'

She gave him a look. 'Yes, there are – and just as obsessed with big boobs.'

Dan blushed and took his arm away. 'Well, that was me back in sixty-six, I'm afraid. Didn't make me stray from my Claire, though, and she was as flat as a board.'

Tracy laughed and took out a tissue to dry her eyes. She forced a smile. 'Do you know, he was the only man to look me straight in the eye when I first arrived here, and when I realised he was also the sweet young guy who used to read me bedtime stories when I was a little girl – well, that was it. What woman wouldn't fall in love with a good-looking doctor there and then?'

Dan had to admit there did seem a certain inevitability to it.

Tracy got her emotions under control and stood up to leave. She gestured towards Dan. 'What Professor Savage has done for you and everyone else in this place is amazing, but you'd think he'd do something else useful while he's at it – like make men think more like women.'

CHAPTER SIX

Alex passed her eyes over the visitors' gallery in the House of Commons. It was busier than usual, which made it difficult to pick out individuals, but he would be there – along with all the other medical experts keen to see history being made.

The Voluntary Euthanasia Bill had just been debated, and when it became apparent that the will of the House couldn't be decided there and then, the Speaker was left with no choice but to call for a vote. Alex pushed the control on her wheelchair and made her way to the Aye Lobby.

Her fellow Members of Parliament parted to give her space as she exited the chamber, but with one of the most controversial bills ever to come before the House to be decided, the Whips had made sure everyone was there, which meant she had little choice but to allow her personal space to become invaded.

Someone took hold of the handles to the back of her wheelchair. It was annoying but, given the situation, Alex decided not to make too much of a fuss.

'I'm quite all right, thank you. I don't require any special treatment.'

The pressure on the handles didn't relent and the unknown transgressor bent down to whisper in her ear. 'Ah, but you're so very special to *me*, Ms Salib.'

Savage's breath reeked of cigars and Alex turned her head away in disgust.

'What are you doing here? You're not a member!'

In a less noisy environment the other MPs might have noticed her distress, but they were too busy discussing their own voting intentions. Alex attempted to get away by accelerating, but the chair refused to move. She pushed the control forward more, but the wheels slipped on the carpet. The professor pushed down on the handles and turned her to face the entrance to the No Lobby. He then placed his cheek against hers, which disgusted her even more.

'Now, are we sure we're making the right decision? What if voting "yes" to euthanasia simply enables those with evil intent to *persuade* the terminally ill to end their lives early?'

Alex tried moving her face away, but his cheek pressed harder. Bristles dug into her skin. She began to fear the agreement they'd reached in his club had some kind of Faustian element to it. Alex became more determined than ever to put an end to his sick practices.

'It's *voluntary* euthanasia and it takes power away from the twisted self-interests of inbreds like you and gives it back to the people.'

Something touched the back of her head and Alex tried not to be sick as the tips of his fingers spread evenly over her scalp. Savage turned to face her as if to ponder the grey matter within.

'Really? I'll remember that as I help the people exercise their *power*.'

The professor took his hand away and stood back up. The space between the two voting lobbies had cleared and clerks prepared to close the doors. Alex needed to be through one of them if she was going to be allowed to vote. Her wheelchair was turned back towards the Aye Lobby and released. She slammed the control forward and entered the voting chamber just as the doors closed behind.

'Stop teasing the new girl, er, trans-whatsit thingy, or whatever she's decided to call herself today.'

Alex took her place in the queue and Savage compared it to the line in the No Lobby.

'Just looking after our interests, Toby. One day, great leaders like the Honourable Alexandra Salib MP will be important to us all.' He glanced at the statue of Baroness Thatcher. 'Very important to us all.'

CHAPTER SEVEN

'Just swipe the screen, Dad – try not to press it.'

Dan tried again, but trembling fingers caused the image to resize instead.

'Damn these hands!'

Lucy took the iPad back from him. 'It's okay, you've only just taken your tablets. They'll be fine in ten minutes. I can do it for you in the meantime.'

The next picture appeared – the cast from a school pantomime, dated 1944. Lucy's mother had centre stage, of course, and Dan grinned.

'Ah, there's my beautiful girl.' He stopped smiling when he saw the prince standing next to her. 'Ritchie Parkes – bastard.'

Lucy grinned instead.

'Talk about ideas above his station – thought he was a real prince when he put that stupid costume on. He wasn't so charming once I'd put chilli powder down his tights, I can tell you.'

His daughter tittered.

'Cinderella might have fallen for royalty in the fairy tale, but after watching him constantly rubbing his balls on the opening night, she soon went for yours truly instead.'

Lucy laughed and pretended to admonish him. 'Dad, that's a horrible thing to do!'

Her father affected indignation in return. 'Well, he was annoying.' Dan motioned for her to swipe to the next picture. 'We renamed him "Itchy Parts" after that.'

Lucy broke into a fit of hysterics and had to put the tablet down. She appeared to need time to recover, so Dan picked up the iPad to see if he could continue the trip down memory lane himself. The tremors were easing, but his hands still shook and the next image in the sequence appeared more by luck than judgement.

It was another promotional shot of *Cinderella* – a solo of Claire this time. He smiled at the memories it brought back. He tried to touch her hair, but ended up zooming into the sash she was wearing instead. Another attempt had the shot panning to the right. He tutted and put the pad back down on his lap. Dan nudged his daughter.

'Have you quite finished? Some of us have sixty years to catch up on, you know.'

Lucy wiped away her tears. 'Dad. I think we'd better lay down some ground rules first – I'll operate the iPad as long as you don't make any more jokes.'

Dan regarded her as if she had just asked the fox not to enter the hen house any more. Sure enough, each image viewed from then on was accompanied by a comment from Dan, which invariably had Lucy needing more time to recover. Her father had always been a raconteur, but this was the first time he'd been able to exercise it in years. Even when Dan knew his witticisms had fallen flat, Lucy still laughed which just encouraged more bad jokes, of course – until the chronological order of the photographs passed 1966.

Dan fell silent and the mood changed. Lucy had been careful to place every family occasion, from birthdays to weddings, consecutively, to help him recall the last six decades, but none of it meant anything after 1966. It wasn't that he didn't recognise his family or himself – the natural ageing of all concerned was perfectly acceptable. No, it was the events themselves and the passage of time between that made something else more evident.

Everything from the advent of colour around the turn of the seventies to the changing clothing fashions, cars, and even buildings in the background – all of it made him realise how much more than just memories Alzheimer's had cost him. It was as if that part of his life had been consumed too.

Dan viewed an image that should have reminded him of the pride and joy he must have felt at the time – standing next to his daughter on her wedding day in 1981. The only comment he could muster was to say how much she looked like her mother on their wedding day. He broke down when Lucy told him it was the same dress.

'We can stop if you want to, Dad.'

Lucy put an arm around her father. Dan couldn't talk, but motioned for her to continue with the photographs. She gave him a tissue and did. Later images depicted just Claire and him – particularly after they retired in 1995. Travel featured and the historical nature of the locations helped Dan to start commenting again, but only because he knew of them prior to 1966. The Pyramids, Taj Mahal, Great Wall of China – happy times.

But then photographs of Claire and Dan's last five years together appeared, and these were very different. It was difficult to see to begin with, as Dan was making an effort to hide what he must have known was coming. An exaggerated smile here, a convenient prop of some kind there, but the early signs of his Alzheimer's could still be seen – particularly in the light of what he knew now.

Dan fell silent again as the photographs progressed to show more visible indications – others in the picture having to point out the camera to him. Everyone smiling while he just stared. Other more practical difficulties emerged and with increasing severity. A walking stick. A wheelchair. A bib around his neck. The cup with two handles on the table. None of it came as a surprise, but what did upset Dan was the accelerated ageing. Not in him – in his wife.

The effect of Dan's dementia on Claire matched his deterioration. In every picture prior to 2016, he could still see the fourteen-year-old beauty he first fell in love with, but not afterwards. Like him, she initially tried to keep up the pretence of normality but, whereas he eventually forgot why, she didn't and wouldn't be allowed to. It showed. From forced smiles to the gradual lack of interest in her own appearance, the stress he put upon her increased.

She even stopped dyeing her hair. Probably because Dan was no longer capable of recognising who she was, let alone of appreciating her crowning glory any more.

If Alzheimer's had aged him prematurely, the burden of being his carer had done something far worse to her. It was as if Death had been determined not to be cheated out of any suffering, so had forced Claire to endure the pain Dan could no longer feel, as well as her own. Dan was wrong about God and the Devil. They were both evil.

There must have been pictures taken the day of her funeral, but he understood why Lucy hadn't included any. The last of the photographs were of him on his own or with Lucy and Tony, but Dan didn't want to see them. He took hold of his daughter's hand.

'Tell me the truth. How did your mother die?'

Lucy tried to reassure him. 'Just old age, Dad. She had a couple of minor strokes and died of a heart attack two months later.'

Dan accepted it, but knew Claire had been forced to suffer years of agony before that. He stared at the wall opposite.

'Are you okay, Dad?'

'Hmmm? Yeah, I'm fine. Just thinking about your mother.'

Lucy placed the iPad as a picture frame next to his bed and set it to display a slide show of the photographs.

She had intended to show them all, but thought 1944 to 1966 would be best.

CHAPTER EIGHT

It was just by chance that Doctor Adams happened to be standing in reception when they arrived. He assumed the occupant of the wheelchair travelling up the ramp to be an outpatient, but the entourage following behind made him realise the hospital was about to be subject to an unannounced inspection. He told the duty receptionist to inform Professor Savage's PA.

The doctor seemed to be the most senior person present, so Alex made a beeline for him. 'My name's Alexandra Salib MP and these people are representatives of the Parliamentary Health Committee, Care Commission, and other legal bodies. We wish to inspect the premises, as allowed under the relevant section of the Health Act. Tell Professor Savage I want to see him.'

She held up her parliamentary ID, which Adams appeared to take his time reading. He eventually handed it back. 'Sir John has been informed. I'd be grateful if everyone could provide reception with their personal details.'

Alex had anticipated such a response. 'No need. The team leaders have already completed the necessary paperwork.'

Six members of the inspection body approached the desk to hand over the information. Alex opened a map of the hospital – the corresponding six areas were marked on it.

'The heads of these departments need to be here as soon as poss—' She was interrupted by the appearance of Savage.

'Ah! My dear Alex! What a very pleasant surprise, and may I be one of the first to congratulate you on your stunning victory yesterday – a historic moment for the country indeed.'

The professor didn't appear to be in the least bit concerned with what usually lay behind an unannounced inspection.

'I didn't introduce the Voluntary Euthanasia Bill, Professor, and you know full well we lost it.'

'Really? Now that *is* disappointing. What must our elected peers have been thinking to actually deny the democratic wish of the people? You must continue to fight the good fight to ensure justice is done.' He continued to grandstand. 'To be part of such a vital step forward in the future of the people can only reflect well on those who enable it, and I'm sure the crucial part you play will not go unnoticed.'

He loomed over her.

'My only hope is that nothing unforeseen should come along and spoil it all. Nature's laws of unintended consequences can be most unforgiving – don't you think?'

Alex ignored what was plainly an attempt to delay.

'Escort one of the teams and me to this department.' She raised the map. Savage gave it a cursory inspection.

'Of course! But all in good time. Surely you must be in need of some refreshment after your long journey. Tea? Coffee? Something stronger, perhaps? I have an excellent twenty-five-year single malt just waiting for the right excuse.'

Alex had only been there five minutes and already she'd had enough of his bullshit. She pushed the map into his stomach. 'Take us there. *Now*.'

The professor motioned for the lift doors to be opened, and stood to one side for her to pass. He deposited the map into a bin as she did.

'Not the elevator,' said Alex. 'I may as well assess the suitability of access while I'm here.'

She headed towards a door marked with the logo of a wheelchair and her team followed. So did two police officers.

A few descending ramps later and they arrived at the entrance to the research department. Adams went ahead to get the door. Alex stopped as he held it open for her.

'Where's the pad?'

Adams looked at her.

She repeated herself. 'Where's the pad – the button at waist height that opens the door automatically, so the department is accessible to all?'

An uncomfortable silence followed, during which the professor moved between her and the doctor.

'Important as that clearly is, none of our researchers

currently require such a device, but I'm sure that would be quickly rectified should the need arise.'

Alex rounded on him. 'Not good enough. What if I were a new graduate looking to work here? How welcome do you think that would make me feel? It should have been *rectified* years ago.' She turned to her team. 'Make a note of that.'

They exchanged puzzled looks before doing so.

The first room was entered. Test tubes, Bunsen burners, Petrie dishes, and various other bits of apparatus needed for the development and testing of potential cures abounded. Three of the inspection team set about their tasks by questioning the researchers present.

Other doors led from the room and Alex pointed to one of them. 'What's in there?'

'That's the cold room. It's where we store what we do here.'

'And just what do you *do* here, Professor?'

Savage scanned those present. 'I'm afraid I'm not at liberty to discuss the exact nature of that, as it's still classified, but I can assure the member for Brighton Pavilion, a public announcement is imminent.'

She indicated the other door. 'And what goes on in there?'

'In there? Oh, that's just where we keep the animals.'

Alex's resolve firmed as the reason for the inspection drew near. 'And just what do you *do* to those poor creatures, Professor Savage?'

Savage placed a hand under the opposite elbow and stroked his chin while he appeared to ponder that.

'I suppose we're currently subjecting them to extreme temperatures.'

Alex snapped an order to her team. 'Get in there – *now!*'

The police officers moved closer to the professor while the instruction was followed. Alex could sense a tremendous justice was about to be dispensed, and turned to enjoy the look on the professor's face as it happened. Annoyingly, he seemed bemused.

The team burst into the room just in time to stop a technician from disposing of what looked to be evidence into a furnace. One of the policemen grabbed what was in the man's hand. It was a plastic bag containing a dead rat – frozen solid. He passed it to his colleague, who wrinkled his nose before handing it over to Alex.

It fell to the floor when she realised how cold it was. That and all the empty cages in the room confused her. Savage walked over to a chest freezer and opened it. He reached in and took out a similarly preserved animal. He then spoke as if Alex wasn't there.

'It was during our meeting in my club that I first realised the Honourable Alexandra Salib MP is not the kind of person to suffer fools. When she said: "Not if the research involves animals, abuse of the unborn, or any other creature unable to make its own decision", I knew then she meant exactly that and wouldn't tolerate anything else. Which is why I gave immediate instructions for all such testing to cease both here and in all other facilities over which I have control.'

Savage raised the deceased rodent up to his face, as if to confirm its condition. 'Sadly, we weren't able to find good homes for them all and, I regret to say, humane euthanasia, followed by the appropriate health and safety legislation, became the only alternative.' He peered through the transparency and into the half-open eyes of the gently thawing cadaver. He kissed it. 'Sweet dreams, Cecil.'

The body was then tossed unceremoniously into the still-open furnace. Savage clasped his hands together. 'Now! Who's for a glass of quarter-century Glenmorangie?'

Alex was rattled, but more convinced than ever that the professor's arrogance belied a genuine enjoyment of suffering, and evidence of it would be in the hospital somewhere.

'Where are they, Professor?'

The look of bemusement returned. 'I'm sorry?'

'The *live* animals you conduct your evil experiments on.'

The assumption Savage was somehow in league with the Devil seemed to encourage yet more theatrical behaviour. 'Evil? I say, isn't that putting it a little strongly? I will admit my work does cause a great deal of stress and anxiety to the poor things, but the satisfaction I get from that cannot be ignored.'

Savage appeared to be mad as well as bad.

Alex glanced at the two police officers and pounced on the apparent confession. 'So you admit to deliberately causing pain and suffering?'

The professor appeared to bow to inevitability. 'I'm afraid so.'

The superior of the two officers spoke. 'We're still going to need evidence, Ms Salib.'

Savage's face lit up. 'And you shall have it! I simply adore showing off what we do here – follow me!'

Alex wondered if his eccentric behaviour masked some kind of denial. Savage strode back through the laboratory and held the door open for them all to leave. They filed past his unbroken smile.

Alex again insisted on using the ramps which meant that by the time they had travelled four floors up, everyone was out of breath apart from her and the professor. Nothing seemed to curtail his enthusiasm. He led them through the geriatric ward and into the conservatory at the far end. He stood in the middle of it.

'Ladies and gentlemen, welcome to my laboratory of *live* animals.' Savage looked down his nose at Alex. 'Although, I prefer the term *human beings* myself. I find they respond so much better to treatment when referred to that way.'

Alex scanned the old-aged pensioners around her. 'What are you up to, Professor?'

He cocked his head to one side. 'My job. You made your requirements perfectly clear and I have complied with them.' He closed the distance to her and bent down to whisper. Alex grimaced and twisted her head away. 'Just as I know you will mine.'

Savage stood back up and turned to the police officers. 'Gentlemen, I do believe you require evidence of the suffering I have caused these good people. Please feel free to ask each in turn for details of the horrors I have deliberately inflicted upon them. I'm sure you will find it most enlightening.'

The senior officer approached Alex. 'Ms Salib, the arrest warrant only covers the 1986 Animals Act. Even if someone is prepared to make an accusation against Sir John, it would need to be investigated first.'

Alex's blood boiled. She approached one of the patients. 'Is it true? Has this man deliberately hurt you?'

The old man placed a hand on her knee, and spoke slowly.

'You're in a hospital, dear. Everything's going to be all right.'

The sound of Adams and the inspection team attempting to suppress their mirth didn't exactly calm Alex. The professor knelt beside the patient.

'How do you do? My name is Professor Sir John Savage and this is the Honourable Alexandra Salib MP. She and her colleagues have been tasked to inspect the hospital, and she's keen to know details of the pain you've suffered during your treatment.'

The geriatric looked at them both before furrowing his brow. 'It's a hospital – pain is as good as guaranteed.'

Alex sighed at what seemed to be another humiliation at the professor's hands. Ever the professional, she covered her embarrassment by taking a politician's interest in the old man's condition. He explained it to her while the inspection team and the police officers prepared to leave.

The patient had said something interesting which made Alex question some of the other patients in the same way. She turned back to her nemesis. Her mood hadn't just improved – she was smiling.

'You lied, Sir John. These poor people arrived here with Alzheimer's disease and at a stage which made it impossible for them to personally agree to their treatment.' She emphasised her point by repeating the last part of the demand she'd made in the professor's club: '*Or any other creature unable to make its own decision.*'

Alex knew the police wouldn't be interested as the relatives would have had powers of attorney but that didn't stop Savage from seizing yet another opportunity to play-act. He dropped his chin to his chest and put his hands out to the officers, as if to offer them a chance to handcuff him. He looked up and left for a moment.

'What's the phrase? Oh yes.' He dropped his head again. 'It's a fair cop.' He half-raised his head and squinted out of one eye. 'I've heard the tea is particularly good in prison but, alas, not the whisky.'

Alex manoeuvred her wheelchair passed him and made for the exit. 'Joke all you want, Professor, but you haven't complied with my requirements after all, which means I don't have to comply with yours either. Good day.'

The professor stood and watched Alex's departure in silence. Dan wheeled his chair up to him.

'Sir John?'

The professor looked down to see where the voice was coming from.

'I just wanted to say on behalf of everyone here, thank you for what you've done for us.' Dan didn't know why the visiting MP appeared to miss the importance of the professor's work but, nevertheless, wanted to show how much it was still appreciated by them all.

Savage smiled at his lab rat. 'That's quite all right, Cecil. Think nothing of it.'

CHAPTER NINE

'I feel sick.' Dan took off what appeared to be a thick sleep mask. 'What did you call this?'

Tony read what was on the box. '"Virtual Reality Glasses" – VR glasses for short.'

'What's wrong with the glasses I've got?'

Tony chuckled. 'These will do much more than help you read, Dan. You can watch movies, play games, tour famous places, you name it. They're perfect for staving off boredom while you're stuck in here.'

Dan tried not to seem ungrateful. He liked Tony and assumed he always had. Lucy and he certainly appeared happy together, but Dan got the impression younger generations didn't just use technology, they relied on it, and he wasn't sure if that was a good thing or not.

'I thought these portable televisions did all that.' He pointed to the iPad by his bed, still steadily flicking through the old photographs.

Tony tried to convert him. 'They do, but this way you get to see everything in *3D reality* – like you're really there. How do you fancy a go on a rollercoaster?'

Dan didn't, but after the effort his son-in-law had

gone to, thought it rude not to show at least some interest.

Lucy put another sense of reality on the situation. 'Don't worry, Dad. It's Tony's latest toy. I'm sure he'll enjoy spending hours playing with it, even if you don't.'

Her husband pursed his lips at her.

Dan put the glasses back on and ignored the mild nausea they caused. He was presented with an image that suggested he was sitting in the front carriage of a switch-back. The scenery and track stretched away in front of him and he acknowledged it did indeed seem real.

'Move your head around, Dan.'

He did as Tony asked and was amazed to see the view extended to the left and right too. Dan turned his stiff neck as far as it would allow, but couldn't see the edge of the picture anywhere. He looked up and down – same result.

Tony enthused. 'A complete three-hundred-and-sixty-degree view in all directions. Imagine if you were wearing a pair of earphones playing sounds at the funfair – you'd think you were there.'

Dan had to admit it was impressive. He looked down at his feet, but couldn't see them. He raised a hand in front of his face, but couldn't see that either.

Tony answered the obvious question. 'I'm afraid you can only view what's on the screen in the glasses – not right through it.'

Dan was a little disappointed. The rollercoaster began to move along the track, and was soon whizzing along typically steep curves, climbs and descents. He unconsciously leaned side to side with the carriage which made him smile – but not for long.

The rollercoaster came out of a loop and Dan stopped smiling, took off the glasses, and vomited in Tony's lap. He wiped his chin on the tissue his daughter had ready and passed the glasses back to her husband.

'Thanks, but no thanks.'

Lucy looked at her other half deciding where best to start and tried not to enjoy his distress too much.

CHAPTER TEN

'I thought that was a lovely thing you did yesterday.'

Dan looked up from his iPad to see Alice being parked beside him. Her appearance took him aback. For someone eleven years into their second century the change was remarkable – positively radiant. Her recovery from dementia didn't make her look any younger, but certainly made Dan think the professor deserved more than his thanks, and told her so.

'It was the least I could do. The guy deserves a peerage, if you ask me. Just think what the end of Alzheimer's disease will mean to the lives of literally billions of people. And I'm not just talking about those with the disease itself – carers, too.'

A picture of Claire appeared on the iPad for a few seconds, and Dan wished they'd both been born ten years later. The next image took its turn in the sequence – standing outside their first home together.

'Is that your wife?'

Dan nodded. He tried to swipe the screen to show Alice a studio portrait of Claire, but the device refused to exit the slideshow.

Alice seemed to sense his frustration. 'I know. My

great-grandson has one of those things and insists that because it can do more than a photograph album, it's somehow better, but give me a snap you can hold in your hand any day. How are you supposed to put that into a locket?'

She reached round the back of her neck and pulled a chain up and over her head to reveal a silver heart-shaped pendant at the end of it. She prised the two halves apart and offered it to him. 'My first husband – killed at Ypres.'

Dan studied the traditional black and white image of a mustachioed gentleman in uniform. A lock of hair resided under a pane of glass in the other half. Dan would have given anything for a lock of Claire's hair.

'I've been married five times since then, but you never forget your first love.'

Dan chuckled. 'I wondered where that glint in your eye came from. Six marriages! The professor and you should be ennobled together.'

Alice glanced at the entrance to the conservatory as if willing someone to walk through it. 'Well, he does have a certain something about him.'

Dan burst out laughing. 'Got to hand it to you, girl, you certainly think life is for living!'

She gave him a look that implied it was her business to put men in a particular order and, if the professor wasn't available, Dan could well be the next most suitable candidate on her list. He winced inside and changed the subject.

'That MP didn't seem very impressed with him, for some reason.'

Alice's response indicated she didn't stray far from her vocation for long. 'Oh, *her*. She has no chance with him. I can tell he's the kind of caring gentleman who would have tried to let her down gently, but you know how some women can be.'

Dan didn't. He'd only known Claire and, if he were to be honest, became uncomfortable when alone with members of the opposite sex, and, even though there were others around, he felt just as intimidated now.

'Of course, all disabled people should be suffocated at birth.'

Dan's mouth fell open. He considered laughing politely at what he thought was a tasteless joke, but her expressionless face suggested something far more serious – Alice seemed to want to put her fantasy love rival down, and not just verbally. If he had any doubts about that, she soon removed them.

'Nature can be cruel to many people and in so many ways, and the sooner their misery is ended, the better.' She leaned forward as if to confide in him. 'Medical men like Sir John are capable of expressing kindness in many ways.'

Dan was lost for words. For a moment, he wondered if she'd switched sides between global conflicts and one of her husbands had been a Nazi eugenicist. He didn't want to get into an argument, so tried reverse psychology instead.

'Many people would say nature has been cruel to *us*, Alice. Do you think Sir John should express his *kindness* towards you and me too?'

She appeared to consider it before breaking into a smile that, in light of her shocking comments, made her look far more monstrous than any illusion he'd had of her.

'He has, Dan.' Her eyes passed over the other patients. 'We're the chosen ones.'

A nurse brought Alice's tablets over and Dan breathed a sigh of relief. Of course. Just like Gary's ramblings of subservient contentment earlier, her treatment was a work in progress too. Surgery involving the brain must cause many more psychological anomalies than just hallucinations – temporary, albeit extreme, changes in personality had to be expected too. Especially with Alzheimer's.

Dan admonished himself for being so quick to jump on the treatment as a done deal, just because he appeared to have been cured. Maybe he'd gone through a similar personality change and was just as unaware of it as Alice and Gary? No – Lucy would have said something.

Alice decided to take the pills in her room and the nurse wheeled her away. Dan realised he still had her locket and went to call her back, but they'd already left the conservatory. He was wondering what to do with it when the lady with the love of television drama caught his eye.

She waved for Dan to join her, which took him straight back to when she'd confused his questions about the aircraft crash with a soap opera she'd been watching at the time. Dan hesitated, but decided she had to be as compos mentis as the rest of them by now. And anyway, he was curious to see if another sweet little old lady had inadvertently been turned into a temporary racist or something.

She pointed at Alice's pendant as he drew up next to her. 'May I have a look?'

Dan passed it over and she opened it.

'Did she tell you this was a picture of her husband?'

'Her first of six! Not bad, eh? One hundred and eleven next month too!'

'If the photograph is from the Great War and is of who she says it is, then she would have to be a lot older than that.'

Dan did the calculation – she was right. The locket must have belonged to Alice's mother, in which case the picture would have to be of her father, and not her first husband. He felt sorry for her again.

'You're Dan, aren't you? How do you do; my name's Nadira.'

Dan was embarrassed. Not only did her maths prove dementia no longer featured in her life but, unlike him, she'd remembered her manners, too. He shook her outstretched hand and tried to make amends.

'Nadira's a lovely name. Where's it from?'

She told him – along with her life story – and when it started with how each set of grandparents met, Dan scoured the room for a polite excuse to escape.

Tracy entered the conservatory and he tried to catch her eye. He missed it. It wouldn't have been so bad if Nadira had paid him any attention while she nattered away but, to add insult to injury, she kept on looking at the television. Nadira actually had the nerve to say *'Shush!'* when something of interest to her appeared on it. At least it shut her up for a few seconds. Dan looked to see what was so important.

It seemed like decades since he'd last watched a television, and he certainly didn't care for soaps, but when Dan recognised the person being featured, he gave it his full attention. The programme was about voluntary euthanasia and how a recent parliamentary vote on the legalisation of it had failed. The interviewer was talking to the very same visiting dignitary from the day before – Alexandra Salib MP. Dan was just becoming interested in her diatribe of words like 'dinosaurs' and 'out of touch' when Nadira began talking again. Any notion he had of her being a polite little old Indian lady evaporated.

'Well, that's it then. May as well cut my wrists now.'

Dan was tempted to say *Shush!* to her too, but thought better of it. He tried to catch Tracy's eye again to see if he could get her to increase the volume, but then stopped himself – not because he'd lost interest in what the MP had to say on the subject of a *good* death, but because Nadira's words worried him.

'I'm ninety-nine years old. No family. No future. No life. So what's the point in going on? If the government's not prepared to end it, then I will.'

As a recent suicide risk himself, Dan had sympathy, even empathy for her words, but they still shocked him – her recovery couldn't have been as advanced as he thought. He attempted to reassure her.

'I know how powerful the feeling of wanting to

take your own life can be, Nadira, but, trust me, I went through exactly the same torment and it's just a phase of the treatment. Once the red pill has done its work, you'll be fine. I promise.' He wondered if she was on a suicide watch.

'Leave 'er alone.'

A walking stick prodded Dan's chest. He looked along its length to see a man he didn't know at the other end.

'Nad 'n' me are goin' to Dignitas, aren't we, darlin'?'

Dan's instinct was to snatch the walking stick out of the stranger's hand, but thought better of it, as that would most likely end with the two of them fighting on the floor. Not with each other, but for breath. He made a more dignified approach and put out his hand.

'I don't believe we've met – my name's Squadron Leader Dan Stewart.'

'Piss off, ponce. Go 'n' find your own gurl to die wiv'.'

Dan could see he was about to be assaulted with the stick again but felt he had no choice this time – he grabbed it. Dan was both relieved and pleased to see it come away from the geriatric thug's hand, who promptly collapsed back into a chair. A clutched chest and look of discomfort did worry Dan but much to his relief, it then turned back to a scowl, allowing him to enjoy the moment – but not for long. The stick was snatched out of Dan's hand and he looked up to see Tracy holding it.

'Bully! Why don't you hit him over the head while you're at it?'

She gave the stick back to its owner. Dan seethed. He attempted to redress the situation.

'If you women made use of the fabled eyes in the back of your head, you'd have seen him attack *me* with it first!'

Tracy ignored him and did what any nurse would do – go to the aid of the person most in need. Dan was about to comment on the unfairness of that when Nadira reached over to console the assailant too. Dan groaned. Justice was never going to be his.

The petty incident aside, both Nadira and her uncouth boyfriend's words made Dan think potential suicide was perhaps the most troubling aspect to the cure for Alzheimer's disease. Hallucinations and personality changes were one thing, but taking your own life before the treatment had had a chance to work was clearly far more serious. What was the point of a miracle that restarted life, only for the recipient to then end it? He wondered what the 'Dig…' thing was.

He spotted Alice being pushed back into the conservatory and went to retrieve her pendant. It was being held out to him.

'Thank you, Nadira.'

She held on to his hand. 'Who's Nadira?'

For a second, Dan questioned whether she'd even had surgery, let alone the medication. He dismissed her question as a one-off and made his way over to the locket's owner. He was rewarded with a smile as he handed it back. Although her earlier comments about Alex Salib had been unacceptable, Dan still pitied Alice, and wondered who the person in the photograph was.

'Alice, it's your one-hundred and eleventh birthday soon. You weren't even born when the First World War started, so that person couldn't possibly be your husband.'

She regarded him with the same look he gave Nadira.

'Alice? You're confusing me with my daughter. I'm her mother, Elizabeth.'

CHAPTER ELEVEN

'Tell me what you're up to.'

Savage looked at the top right-hand corner of *The Daily Telegraph*. 'Page eleven apparently.'

'You know perfectly well what I'm talking about. When a significant number of stock market shares are bought unexpectedly in one particular sector, people take notice. Especially when that sector has nothing whatsoever to do with the purchaser's expertise or insider knowledge.'

The professor gave the Secretary of State for Business his full attention. 'Well, thanks to your ridiculously restrictive laws, I'm forbidden from making significant investments in my own companies, so forced to look elsewhere to supplement a meagre pension.'

The Right Honourable Tarquin Asquith-Bennington MP had known Professor Sir John Savage, KBE FRCS FMedSci, since they were at Eton together, and even though they'd always been close – very close at one time – thought him to be just as enigmatic now as he was then. The Business Secretary expanded on what he knew.

'Nevertheless, to purchase shares in nearly every major online media company, and in amounts deliberately designed not to cause any sudden price movements, means you know something. Even some of the pseudonyms you used to hide the transactions are new – or at least the ones my spies have managed to identify are.'

Savage folded the newspaper and placed it on the occasional table between them. 'Still plenty of opportunity for you to invest too, Tarquin.'

They were interrupted by the club steward. Both ordered single malts. Tarquin adopted a different approach.

'What I don't understand is, you're a complete Luddite when it comes to social media. You don't even have a LinkedIn account, let alone Facebook or Twitter, and yet you've bought nearly ten million dollars' worth of shares in each – Google too.'

The professor extended an index finger and pointed it towards the ceiling of the club. The minister narrowed his eyes at it.

'Twenty million?'

The professor didn't respond and the forefinger stayed where it was.

'Please don't tell me you spent over one hundred million dollars on something you know absolutely nothing about?'

Savage remained stoic, as did the finger. The business secretary's jaw went slack. 'John, where on earth did you get that kind of money? More to the point, how did you manage to hide it? I can see I'm going to have to fire a few people – you do realise what would happen if you were to suddenly dump that lot?'

The professor reassured him. 'Calm yourself, Tarquin. Forget the amount – think of it more as one putting one's money where one's mouth is. I'm sure you and the rest of the Asquith-Benningtons will come to appreciate it.'

The minister had known the professor for long enough to be able to trust his word in all things medical, and even some business, but when it risked destabilising stock markets then that was a different matter. Even investigating what he'd done could trigger a crash, let alone a sudden disposal of the shares. Tarquin had always been a little intimidated by his friend but felt vulnerable now, too. He hoped it didn't show and changed the subject.

'Anyway, how's the trial going?'

The professor sighed. 'Not as well as I'd hoped. We've already lost one test subject and another is expected to expire in the next week or so. Ms Salib is proving to be a challenge too.'

Tarquin became puzzled. 'Why are you even bothering with her? If the initial results of the cure for Alzheimer's are as promising as you say, then the health committee's bound to agree to widen the trial. You don't need her blessing for that.'

'Just keeping our enemies close, Tarquin. And, anyway, I want to try and help her professionally.'

Tarquin sneered. 'Well, she's certainly not helping you. In fact, she appears to make it her business to do the exact opposite. Did I hear she tried to get you shut down for animal cruelty the other day?'

'She's principled, I'll give her that. Ended our little agreement on the spot when she discovered the test subjects were unable to give *personal* consent to their treatment, for goodness' sake.'

His friend was still perplexed. 'Since when did you feel the need to be so generous with someone who openly despises everything you stand for?'

Savage glanced around the room. 'Tarquin, I'm sorry to have to say, we live in times where clear majorities in the House of Commons are a thing of the past, so compromises with our enemies have to be made. Now, if that means pandering to individuals we would much rather ignore, then so be it. Extending the trial into care homes is not the issue, but getting approval for the next stage will prove ethically difficult for some, and cross-party support will be essential.'

He drew closer. 'If the public thinks voluntary euthanasia is controversial, wait until they discover what the cure for Alzheimer's disease *really* means.'

The steward placed two glasses of whisky and a jug of water on the table. The Business Secretary poured a few drops from it into each drink while pondering the professor's share acquisitions. There had to be a connection with the clinical trial, but he was damned if he could think what it was.

CHAPTER TWELVE

Dan reached for the teacup but collapsed back into his chair when he saw who was sitting opposite him. He grabbed at his chest. 'Don't do that! I almost had a heart attack!'

Brian looked at the picture of Claire on the iPad between them. 'Isn't that what you want?'

Dan tried putting the thought out of his head. At least the reappearance of his brother's hallucination confirmed the treatment needed more time.

Brian perked up. 'Ninety-six years of age, eh? Now, there's a turn up for the books!'

Dan tilted his head towards the ceiling. 'Well, let's test my new memory, shall we? What were the words you used? Oh yes. "Your brain has conjured up a hallucination to *help*." A fat lot of good you've been – couldn't even get my age ri—' He trailed off when he realised others in the conservatory were looking at him.

'*We* couldn't get *our* age right. One and the same – remember?'

Dan didn't want to draw attention to himself again, so he asked Brian if it was possible to communicate by thought alone. The hallucination tutted.

'Of course we can. I'm in your head – or have you forgotten that, too?'

Tracy approached and Dan realised it wasn't just *his* spoken words they could all hear and see – Brian's came out of his mouth, too. Dan just had time to tell his illusion to shut up, when she addressed him.

'Brian?'

Dan tried to think of an excuse for the apparent relapse, but couldn't. 'It's okay, Tracy, I'm just having a conversation with my brother, er, I mean my hallucination.' Dan's face flushed with embarrassment, but he couldn't see how else to tackle it.

Her reply surprised him.

'That's okay; it means you're well on the way to a full recovery.' Tracy smiled and patted him on the shoulder.

Dan asked Brian what he thought she meant by that. The lips on his hallucination didn't move as it replied.

'Beats me. Maybe hallucinations are part of the treatment and not just a side-effect.'

Dan thought that was an interesting point, and pondered it while studying the other patients in the room. Alice no longer had her doll, but was clearly still in communication with what she thought was her mother. She, or it, had even spoken to him. Nadira had something similar going on, and there was Gary. He seemed happy with who he was, though – a bit too happy for Dan's liking, but the apparent change in both his and Alice's personalities implied something more than just illusion. Schizophrenia perhaps? Maybe it was that which caused the thoughts of suicide in Nadira and her plebeian boyfriend.

Brian made another one of his less helpful suggestions. 'You know, up until now I've always assumed I was *your* hallucination. What if you were mine?'

Dan scoffed. 'That's nearly as good as the one about me being a factory worker. Nowhere near as funny, though.'

Brian persisted. 'My words came out of your mouth just now – she even called you "Brian".'

Dan was irritated by the nonsense. 'That's because my episodes with you are well-documented – all the staff know about *my* hallucinations of *you*.'

Brian looked down at the iPad again. 'Lucy certainly did an excellent job with that slideshow. A complete history going right back.' He stared at Dan. 'Funny how I'm not in any of them.'

CHAPTER THIRTEEN

'Try this – it's my own special blend.'

Alex peered at it with suspicion. 'Sunita, your straight stuff is good enough. No need to risk a bad trip caused by whatever you've concocted.'

Sunita spoke as if she were Alex's GP. 'Are you in pain?'

They both knew the answer to that.

'Then smoke it.'

Alex had always known pain. Second only to championing the weak and vulnerable, her whole life was about the control of it. Ever since she could remember, hardly a year went by without being diagnosed with some new condition that either caused or added some further agony. Congenital paraplegia, quadriplegia, tetraplegia – they all seemed to form some kind of cruel promotion, just for her. Why did she have to suffer so much? It would make sense if her brain had a reason for choosing to interpret the signals it received in the way it did.

The mind inside was a different matter, however – cognitively unaffected, and razor sharp. She even surprised herself at the speed at which she could demolish her opponents, particularly on the floor of the House of Commons. She knew, of course, a significant part of that was down to her impairments – a collective pity for Alex's condition made it difficult for even the most ardent of adversaries to triumph over her. They always ended up looking like bullies.

But this success came with what all impairees have to put up with – the frustration of the unimpaired regarding them with sympathy rather than mutual respect. Alex regarded it as a weakness in the so-called able-bodied and, as any politician knows, weaknesses are there to be exploited. Especially your own.

In any case, it was becoming evident that the combination of a useless body and brilliant mind produced a strength far greater than the sum of the parts and that made her potentially unstoppable in politics. It might be unethical to use impairment to one's advantage, but plenty of other women used their so-called assets for similar purposes, and history was littered with men abusing positions they were born with, so why not her? As long as the cause was genuine, anything could be justified. She saw her condition as a metaphor for the suffering of a world that only she understood and knew how to save. Alex had little time for religion but, if someone were to say she was the chosen one, then perhaps her own physical challenges really would start to make sense.

Chronic pain was still a barrier to ambition, though, and when Alex's legal prescriptions ceased giving her relief from it, she always turned to Sunita for help.

They had first met as patients during one of Alex's many hospitalisations, and, when a shared interest in saving the Earth as well as the use of some of its more natural remedies became apparent, struck up a relationship. Alex knew Sunita could be relied upon to come up with something – all illegal, of course – and if her colleagues, and especially her enemies, were to find out, well, that would be that. She trusted her, though. She had to.

Alex took a long, slow draw. The effect was almost instant. The pain disappeared. She went to put the joint back to her lips, but ended up bumping fingers against them instead – Sunita had taken the spliff away as soon as the job was done. It would have been let go otherwise.

Alex touched her lips again and then looked at her hand. She rubbed the tips of her thumb and forefinger together and giggled when she realised she could no longer feel them – or anything else for that matter.

She extended one of the digits to Sunita while slurring her words.

'*You* are a very bad person. What you are doing here is illegal, and I'm going to have to close you down.' She put her head back and giggles turned to laughter. Sunita smiled, put the joint to her own lips and chuckled too. It made Alex laugh more.

The initial rush of the drug soon wore off and mellow contemplation replaced the uncontrolled humour. Sunita must have guessed Alex was referring to her recent failure at the neurological hospital.

'There's other ways of smashing the system, Al. You'll find one.'

Alex was becoming sleepy, but wanted to enjoy the pain-free existence for as long as possible, so shook her head to try and stay awake. Sunita's comment had registered and Alex tried to get angry about Savage, but the cannabis wouldn't allow it.

She sighed. 'I hate him, Suni. I detest everything about him. From his stuck-up accent to his posh friends, to his silly bow-tie, to his Frankenstein ideas of getting me walking.' Alex peered at her friend. 'He's both a mad scientist *and* the monster he's created. And, as everyone knows, all monsters must die.'

She put her head back and laughed again. Sunita manoeuvred her wheelchair closer.

'Did he really say he could help you to walk?'

Alex stopped laughing and jolted her head back up. She sensed a weakening in her sister-sufferer's resolve. 'Don't give in to propaganda, Suni. It's all bullshit. Bullshit designed to make us conform to their dystopian ideas of the perfect state: a society of Little Lord Fauntleroys pampered by – guess who?' Alex regarded her underdeveloped and deformed lower limbs. 'Even if he could make these move by themselves, they never grew with me into adulthood, so how's he going to fix that?'

She took the joint, drew another breath, and giggled again. Sunita looked at her own just as useless but fully adult legs.

Alex was becoming used to the cannabis and went to take a third puff, but gave the joint back to her friend instead. She became philosophical.

'Suni, I'm going to do whatever it takes to save this world, and if that means having to get near to a monster before I can kill it, then…'

She broke off as her admirer drew nearer. Their lips met for a few seconds. Sunita offered Alex the spliff, but she just stared at it.

'If the public thinks voluntary euthanasia is controversial, wait until they discover what the cure for Alzheimer's disease *really* means.'

CHAPTER FOURTEEN

Tracy waited for Dan to stop her as she swiped through the photographs but he was no longer paying attention to them. He was staring at his hallucination, still sitting in the chair opposite. Brian raised an eyebrow. Dan addressed his nurse.

'I want to see the medical records.'

Tracy paused before replying, which Dan took as yet another attempt to hide something.

'*All* the files this time, with nothing removed or blanked out.'

Tracy explained what that would entail. 'I'll need to get permission from Doctor Adams first.'

'Do whatever you have to, Tracy. I want to see them.'

She paged Adams and the next thing Dan knew, he was being wheeled to the ward office. He raised a hand as they passed his room on the way. Tracy stopped.

'Did all the patients commence the trial at the same time?'

She confirmed it. He pointed at the door opposite his.

'Then why did he *go home* early?'

Tracy hesitated again, and Dan jumped on it before she had a chance to reply. He mocked her words.

'Did the *lucky thing* commit suicide instead?'

She responded to that immediately, which meant Tracy at least thought she was telling the truth. Maybe she was being lied to, too?

'No, Dan, definitely not. It's true he went through the same suicidal stage as you, but he was bedridden and couldn't possibly have taken his own life. He died of natural causes, I'm afraid – old age.' She knelt down in front of him. 'I'm sorry I had to lie to you before, but your treatment relies on positive thinking just as much as the red pill and, for reasons which must now be obvious, knowledge of anything negative has to be avoided.'

Dan accepted the explanation, but still regarded her with suspicion. 'And what about the patients I haven't seen? What about *Brian*?'

Tracy didn't answer and got up to continue pushing him towards the office. Adams was waiting when they arrived. Dan got out of the wheelchair.

'You once asked me how I would feel if my brother died.' He moved closer to the doctor. '*I've never had a brother and you know it*. I think my hallucination is of a patient who was also on the trial. I want to know what happened to him, along with any others no longer with us.'

Adams pulled open a drawer in the filing cabinet he was standing next to. It contained folders divided into alphabetical order.

'What was Brian's surname?'

Adams glanced at Tracy before replying: 'Passen.'

Dan enjoyed a rare moment of satisfaction with his adversary before reaching for the one and only folder filed under the letter 'P'. The meaning of it struck him.

'*Passen*. My hallucination didn't pick any random letter – I was trying to remember Brian's *surname*. I can't believe I thought it meant *passengers*.'

He pulled the folder out, but Adams put a hand on it.

'You clearly don't remember, but we've been here many times before, and each time you've left vowing never again to take the red pill. What you have to ask yourself is, if ignorance means you will live but the truth means you will die, should it really be known?'

Dan regarded him as if he were mad. 'The truth should *always* be known.'

Dan withdrew the folder from the doctor's hand and read Brian's personal details on the front cover. He looked at the photograph of him.

A pain began in his jaw, passed down through the neck and into his left arm. A sudden tightening in the chest caused him to let go of the folder, which fell to the floor. He became nauseous and felt his legs buckling, so grabbed the open drawer. The cabinet started to topple, but Adams held on to it. The chest pressure merged with the pain in his arm, and he knew he was about to let go, but only needed to see one more thing to confirm what he'd just learned was indeed the truth. The heart attack reached the peak of its agony and he collapsed, but not before confirming there were no folders under the letter 'S'.

CHAPTER FIFTEEN

'Come on, Danny – wake up!'

'Wake up, Dad.' It was his daughter's voice.

Someone took hold of his left hand. For a second, he thought both his wife and daughter must be with him.

'Dad, can you hear me?'

His hand was being caressed. He opened his eyes. Not in the ward office any more. There was a beeping sound.

'Dad, do you recognise me?'

He squinted at the shock of blonde hair. It never ceased to amaze him how much Lucy looked like her mother. Or was it the other way around?

'Where's your mother?' he croaked, before remembering why she couldn't possibly be there.

Lucy didn't answer. He focussed on her and tried to smile.

'Boy, are you a sight for sore eyes. Where am I?'

He scanned the room and saw the hoist, the window, and the calendar. His frustrating iPad was still sitting on the side too – steadily going through Lucy's slideshow, but it was something new that mainly caught his eye. The steady beeping sound came from it.

He answered his own question. 'Back in my room. How did I get here?'

'Try not to stress yourself, you're still very weak.'

There was a knock on the door and Adams entered. He smiled at them both.

'Awake, I see. Good morning. Do you know who I am?'

'Doctor Adams.'

The doctor took his patient's temperature, checked the heart monitor, the various tubes and wires, and then the bandages.

'I'm afraid you're going to be needing all this for a while. Mind if I ask you a few questions?'

Lucy's father knew what was coming and would be answering the same queries in the same way. All except the first one. The answer to that question was going to be very different.

The doctor took out his notepad and poised a pen over it. 'What's your name?'

Brian looked at his daughter. 'Brian Passen.'

Lucy jumped up and down in her seat and squeezed his hand. She apologised when he grimaced.

'And how old are you?'

Brian correctly answered that too, and then all the other questions without even being asked. So that was why he had been lied to. That was why he had to restart the medication and why the red pill had to be given time to work because without it, the truth would have been too dreadful to contemplate.

He wasn't Dan Stewart and he certainly wasn't a squadron leader in the Royal Air Force. He was a plain mister. Mr Brian Passen – retired factory worker.

The session was ended as usual by Adams asking his patient if he had any questions of his own. Brian most certainly did. He went to raise his head to ask them, but the coronary wouldn't let him. Lucy was right as always. He was still very weak; he wondered just how much. Brian asked the first question while still flat on his back.

'Who is Dan Stewart and why did I think I was him?' He didn't give the doctor a chance to answer as he turned to his daughter. 'I suppose you knew who I was all along?'

Lucy gave her father a hug. 'Only for the last sixty-six years.'

Tracy and Tony entered. They smiled at Brian and he groaned.

'I'm fed up with being the last person to know what's going on around here.' He squinted at Adams. 'Anything else you're hiding from me?'

The doctor smiled too and, for a moment, Brian wondered if he was about to have a second cardiac arrest.

'Squadron Leader Daniel Stewart was killed six months ago when the aircraft he was piloting crashed. That's all we know.'

Brian relaxed with satisfaction. 'So, I was right. There *was* an aircraft accident.' He tried lifting his head again, but a tremendous weight seemed to be holding it down. 'Six months ago? Not in 1966?' Everyone in the room nodded. 'Then I must have read it in a paper or seen it on the news when I first arrived, and he stuck in my head for some reason.'

'You couldn't even recognise a newspaper then, Brian, let alone read one – Alzheimer's had seen to that – and, in any case, your daughter and her husband have been trying to find out who he was ever since you first used his name.'

Both Lucy and Tony indicated the fruitlessness of their search.

'So, how did he get into my head?'

The doctor seemed to steel himself for some reason.

'The only reason we know a Daniel Stewart once existed is because he told us.' Adams then appeared to hesitate before adding: 'Through you.'

Brian sneered at this latest attempt to pull the wool over his eyes. 'Come on, Doc, you're the last person I'd expect to believe in ghosts. I'm a retired factory worker, apparently, not a medium!' He appealed to the others for support. They didn't give it.

Adams leaned towards him. 'Professor Savage's procedure involves transplanting more than just *new* brain cells.'

The rate of beeping from the heart monitor increased.

CHAPTER SIXTEEN

'Good afternoon, Father. And how may I be of service to you?'

The Reverend Francis McGee opened his mouth to state the purpose of his visit, but something else came out when he saw what the professor was doing. 'I didn't know you had an interest in tropical fish?'

Savage withdrew a net from the tank and they both looked into it. The hospital's chaplain shook his head at the small, motionless, but colourful body lying within.

'*Liopropoma carmabi* – a Candy Basslet. I'm afraid God takes back even his most beautiful creatures eventually.' He regarded the modest tank and the exotic creatures within it. 'Not to mention the most expensive. You've a small fortune in there – good gracious, the angelfish alone must have cost twenty thousand.' The reverend's expertise appeared to extend to their habitat and he voiced concerns about it. 'I'm sorry, Sir John, but they need a much bigger tank and have to be separated as soon as possible – it's only a matter of time before that parrotfish makes a meal out of them all.'

The professor retrieved the dead fish from the net, picked it up by the tail, and dangled it in front of the carnivore. A creature originally purchased for one thousand pounds sterling was devoured in a single bite.

Father Francis was offered a drink and a seat. He shook his head to the whisky but inched back into the chair, unable to take his eyes off the aquarium. Savage was pleased to see they shared more than just a theological interest. A small Australian flathead swam into the path of the parrotfish while the professor explained his hobby.

'I find tropical fish to be so inspiring. Whenever the inevitable human cost of what I do threatens to question the purpose of my work, I only have to look into that tank at God's own sacrifices and my spirits lift immediately.'

It took the parrotfish two bites this time, but then the flathead had cost two thousand pounds. The reverend raised a finger in the direction of the marine murderer as it appeared to head off in search of more money to eat. The professor got out of his chair and stood between the two of them.

'I know what's worrying you, Father. You're concerned about the patients here.'

The reverend composed himself.

'Ahem. Well, as you know, Sir John, I've been the head chaplain for three years now and like to think my team and I have come to know the spiritual needs of the hospital well. But recently…'

The parrotfish had caught up with the angelfish and snapped onto its tail. Unlike the previous victims, they were of equal size and both men turned to watch the battle that ensued. The chaplain's look of horror reflecting back in the glass just increased Savage's enjoyment of it. The twenty thousand pound challenger soon succumbed and the victor settled down to the bottom of the tank to enjoy a more leisurely meal.

The chaplain appeared shocked, but continued. 'The thing is, I expect to have to deal with difficult sins like suicidal thoughts, but, just recently, there's been a noticeable increase of it in the geriatric ward.' He raised his main concern. 'Some of the patients are even seeking absolution from God, while they make approaches to organisations like Dignitas.' The reverend's next statement seemed to cause him some embarrassment. 'The miracle of the dementia treatment appears to be actually *causing* it.'

'Maybe God thinks it's time to take *those* beautiful creatures back too?'

The reverend became angry and stood up. 'I'm sure you can appreciate the difficult position this puts the Church in, Sir John, not to mention the concerns society will raise once the details are made public.'

The professor dismissed the veiled threat and attempted to put the padre's mind at rest. 'Father, please be assured that what you've witnessed is a difficult but thankfully short-term side-effect of the treatment, and nothing permanent. Once the brain cells I've introduced have fully integrated with the recipient's existing central nervous system, peace and harmony will ensue and everyone's concerns will be allayed.'

The reverend managed a thin smile before being drawn to the sight of the parrotfish, still enjoying its meal. He shuddered. Savage put out a hand.

'Anything else I can do to put your mind at rest, Father?'

He looked at his visitor's forehead, rather than in the eye.

'No, I er, don't think so. Thank you very much for your time.'

He shook the professor's hand and turned to leave. Savage went back to tending his fish.

'Of course, the treatment does raise other, perhaps more interesting, theological questions.'

Father Francis made an about turn. 'Such as?'

The professor picked up the net, dipped it into the water and began searching for something at the bottom of the aquarium. 'Dualism.'

The reverend narrowed his eyes. 'Are we talking about good and evil, heaven and earth, or mind and matter?'

The professor thought for a moment. 'All that and more, I suppose. If I were to transplant a kidney from one patient to another, what would you say that was, from a dualistic point of view?'

A heavy sigh told Savage his visitor was hoping to philosophise on something a bit more thought-provoking. 'I think even non-believers would call that a transfer of matter to matter.'

The professor acknowledged the opinion while continuing his underwater investigations. 'So presumably you view the transplanting of *physical* brain cells from one man into another in exactly the same way?' The reverend nodded. Savage broadened the concept. 'What if I were to tell you that that process also transplants the donor's *conscious mind*?'

Father Francis walked over. 'Then I would say that was still matter to matter, as the mind still exists in the physical cells of the donor.'

The professor was trying to coax his largest fish out of the crevice it was hiding in. 'So, would proof of a person's consciousness existing completely *outside* a physical brain be confirmation of a spirit? A soul perhaps?'

A sympathetic hand was placed on the professor's shoulder.

'John. The only spirit you and I should concern ourselves with, is the holy one. God. The supreme being to whom we must all confess our sins.'

The piranha slipped its moorings and headed out into the tank. Father Francis's eyes widened in horror as it spotted the parrotfish, pounced and tore it to pieces.

'There's always a bigger fish, Father.'

CHAPTER SEVENTEEN

The rate of beeping settled at the higher level.

Brian tilted his eyes up. 'So, let me get this right. There's not only me in here, but somebody else, too?'

Everyone nodded while looking at the heart monitor. A collective sigh of relief resounded as the number of beats per minute reduced again.

Adams continued to explain Brian's treatment. 'It's difficult for neural stem cells alone to repair the damage caused by Alzheimer's disease. Mature, preformed neurons and synapses are also required if the brain is to regain full control of not just basic bodily functions, but higher cerebral activities like reasoning, judgement, and concentration. The problem is, that's all finely associated with consciousness, which inevitably means the donor's actual thoughts passing into the recipient's brain too – they're impossible to separate out.'

Brian stared into space. 'Including memories, I suppose.' A light seemed to go on in his head. 'But Dan's been alive for most of the last four decades, so why can't I recall any of it? Alzheimer's may have robbed my brain of those times, but as a young man, he would have had no problem remembering at least the last thirty.'

The doctor put his notepad and pen away. 'Only a relatively small and select number of his cells were transplanted into you – not his entire brain – and the red pill deals with the psychosis those few memories cause by synchronising them with your existing consciousness. Brian Passen, the retired factory worker, can't remember the last sixty years, not just because of Alzheimer's, but because the medication ensured Dan's memories merged with yours. Even now you're convinced *you* crashed *your* aircraft back in 1966.'

Brian grimaced. 'That's the biggest shock. Finding out I'm not a retired fighter pilot after all – just a boring factory worker.'

Lucy squeezed his arthritic hand. 'You'll always be my hero, Dad.'

Brian didn't know if the tear that formed in his eye came from pain or something more meaningful. The look of love for his daughter turned to puzzlement.

'Dan mistook you for his wife and then his daughter. Did he have any children of his own? Does his widow know what's happened to him?'

The doctor's delay in answering made Brian suspicious again. He went to snap at Adams, but weakness ensured he stayed glued to the bed.

Brian croaked: 'Just tell me the truth, Doctor.'

'We honestly don't know. Next of kin details aren't known when a kidney is transplanted, and brain cells are treated just as anonymously. We only know as much as we do because the squadron leader himself told us. Even if he did have a family, it's clear the treatment made sure it was Claire and Lucy.' The physician became philosophical. 'Assuming, of course, we're still talking about Dan and Brian as two *separate* people. Only one person can answer that.' He took out his notepad and pen again. 'Are they? What can you remember now?'

The patient pondered it carefully. 'I... can... remember...' he said, before lifting his right arm. 'Incredible pain.' He winced at Dan's recollection of flesh being peeled away layer by layer. Brian turned to the room's window, where the sun could be made out through some clouds. 'Trees... grass... flowers.' He looked back towards them all. 'And a bumble bee.'

He smiled. 'I *think* I was once a squadron leader in the Royal Air Force named Dan Stewart, who became a retired factory worker named Brian Passen.' He glanced at the iPad and then at Lucy again. 'And along the way I married a wonderful woman and had an equally wonderful daughter.'

Brian let the last vestiges of his conspiracy theories slip away and accepted the chimera he'd become.

CHAPTER EIGHTEEN

Lucy was still upset when they got back to the car. Tony hugged and kissed her. He didn't know what to say. What can be said when your wife's just been told a terminal heart condition means that her father's unlikely to survive the week? Doctor Adams' prognosis couldn't be clearer, but Tony still thought blind optimism was best.

'Your dad's always been one hell of a fighter, Lucy. If anyone can get through this, Brian can.'

He kissed her again and they got into the Ford. She pulled down the sun visor and dabbed her running mascara with a tissue.

'I've got to keep reminding myself it's a miracle he can even recognise me, but it seems so cruel to get my dad back just for something else to take him away again.' She stared ahead. 'It'll be like he'll have died *twice*.'

Tony started the engine and began the drive home. They passed a tractor on the way and he shuddered before switching the Focus into self-driving mode.

'I don't think I'll ever look at farm machinery in the same way again.'

Lucy put a hand over her heart and had another go

at him. 'I can't even bear to think about it – *stupid thing to do*! I could have lost you both.' She'd admonished him enough over the last few days, and seemed content to let it rest there. She pulled down her sun visor again. 'Can we stop somewhere? I need to do my make-up.'

Tony entered the location of a roadside café into the satnav and a short while later, the car had parked itself near the entrance. He chose the same table as before and watched the tractor trundle by while Lucy was in the restroom. He thought more about the incident, and felt guilty at just how close to death Brian and he had actually come. He was looking across the table at where his father-in-law had been sitting during their recovery from the shock when Lucy planted herself there.

'Phew! That's better. I can't think straight without my face on.'

Tony smiled. He reached out to take her hand and the tea they'd ordered arrived. Lucy played mum and started pouring, while Tony thought about the last time he'd drank tea in the café.

Yet here I am, in the middle of a real government cover-up.

'Lucy? How do you feel about your father not being *exactly* who he was?'

She was concentrating on not spilling the contents of the teapot, so the question had to be repeated.

'What do you think of your dad being a mixture of *two* people now?'

Lucy put down the pot and reached for the sugar. 'I know it sounds weird, but it hasn't bothered me, to be honest. Up until today, I've just been so happy for him to be able to recognise me again. I know Doctor Adams always warned he would be different, but to be honest, Dad could call himself Joe Bloggs for all I care. Watching his face light up every time I walk into the room after years of having him look straight through me is amazing. Don't you think?'

Tony did, but he was still troubled. He didn't want to add to his wife's upset, so chose his words carefully.

'But he's so *different* now. And what he's remembered compared to what he's forgotten seems strange. I've nothing against this Dan Stewart, but considering how little of his brain was put into your father, it's striking how much like Dan he's become – always assuming that's how Dan was, of course.'

Lucy thought about the changes in her father. It was true that he was different now, but after years of watching Alzheimer's cruelly twist the man's gentleness into a personality of fear and violence, before wrenching it away completely, any decent character would do. Even the awkwardness of having to pretend to be her mother or her six-year-old self again had been worth the stress. She knew what her husband meant, though.

'I must admit I could do without the accent.'

'Accent? That's putting it mildly – he's completely posh now! We may not know who Squadron Leader Stewart actually was, but I bet he voted Tory. The union would be up in arms if they could hear Brian talk today.'

Lucy snapped at him. 'Do you really think I care what a bunch of bitter and twisted old communists from the seventies thinks? We were a very happy family until Dad got involved with them – totally brainwashed him.'

Tony defended the movement and Brian's involvement with it. 'Your father was a hero to the workers back then, and you should be proud of what he and the rest of the shop stewards fought for.' He tapped the table with a forefinger. 'Basic workers' rights.'

'What? You mean the basic right to go on strike because the recession meant some workers had to be laid off? The same right to strike that forced all the workers to then lose their jobs when the factory had to close down? The same *right to strike* that saw us queuing for food parcels while the union celebrated bringing down *posh* people who simply reopened the factory somewhere else? Dad was unemployed for years thanks to those bigots and yet he still paid his membership subs.'

'Exactly! You should be proud of that kind of loyalty. You can't have a society where it's one rule for some and another for others.'

Lucy calmed. 'That's right. Strange how you never saw the union bosses begging for food, though.'

Tony mellowed a little. 'I'm just saying, your dad played a proud and prominent part in the union movement in those days, but it's strange how he only remembers being a worker now – nothing else.'

'Tony, he had Alzheimer's. Up until six months ago he'd forgotten his entire life, let alone a period of history the rest of us just want to forget anyway. He remembers his family and that's the most important thing.' Lucy became sad again. 'You do know he just wants to be with Mum now, don't you?'

Tony nodded and looked out of the window. Their Ford Focus occupied the space where he'd parked the E-type previously.

The designer of that car built it to be the best there is and yet there's always someone who wants it to be better. Imagine if we treated people the same way.

CHAPTER NINETEEN

Tracy threw her arms around Adams and burst into tears. He waited for a reply to his question which she began to give but then stopped, let go, and took out a handkerchief to recover. She wagged a finger at him.

'*Oh no*. You're not getting away with it that easily. I want the full works – romantic meal for two, bended knee and everything. Asking me to marry you in the ward office is about as unromantic as it gets.' She regarded his empty hands with disdain before putting hers on her hips. '*You haven't even got a ring.*'

'I thought we'd choose one together.'

'You're supposed to get it anyway and I decide whether to take it back or not.'

He gave her a look. 'What was that about romance?'

Tracy playfully slapped his shoulder and they embraced again. She ran her fingers through his hair, slowing her movements as she did so – he appeared to be undergoing another one of her special physical examinations.

'What are you looking for this time?'

'Just checking it was you who asked the question.'

Adams laughed. 'And did you find any evidence of the professor's handiwork?'

'No, but I'd still like to know what's finally brought you to your senses.'

'Well, I considered what you said about me being the wrong side of forty and you—'

She put a hand over his mouth. 'Do you want to try that again?'

He nodded and she let him speak. He took her hand. *'I love you and don't ever want to lose you.'*

The nurse half-closed her eyes and wallowed for a moment in the perfect romance of the words – before snapping back to reality and planting a quick peck on his cheek. 'Good boy.'

Adams grimaced – the highly qualified medical professional appeared to have become some kind of pet.

The love of her life finally seeing sense, Tracy moved straight to planning the next stage of their life together. She tousled his greying hair again. 'You're right about your age. We'd better start a family while you're still up to it.'

'What are you talking about? There are decades of healthy sperm production left in me – men can father children well into their nineties.'

'Well, if you're going to be anything like the nonagenarians in here, count me out having sex with you.' Tracy tried to ignore the picture that conjured up in her mind. 'Mind you, thanks to Professor Savage, we're all going to end up living forever anyway.'

Adams considered that. 'He'd have to get around the laws of diminishing returns first. Fixing one problem in geriatrics just seems to cause or highlight another. Take

Brian Passen, for instance. We finally manage to crack his dementia, only for angina to finish him off. It's a bit like an old car – no matter how good the maintenance, sooner or later it's going to have to be replaced with a newer model.'

Tracy pondered the patients' ages. 'Don't you think it's strange the professor chose such elderly subjects for the trial?'

Adams narrowed his gaze at her. 'It's Alzheimer's, Tracy. The disease and old age tend to come hand in hand.'

She continued to make her point. 'Yes, but there are plenty of people in their fifties and sixties living with the early onset of it, so why not choose from them instead? Their secondary conditions are bound to be far less life-threatening. It's almost as if he needed them to be as old as possible. You said yourself you didn't understand why such *physically weak* candidates were selected.' She put her two and two together. 'We've already lost one patient. Maybe he wants them all to die?'

Adams scoffed at the unethical implication of her suggestion, but Tracy stood firm.

'Okay, Mister Know-it-all. You explain it.'

He had to admit he couldn't. Tracy walked over to a filing cabinet and pulled open a drawer. She took a folder from it.

'I wonder if there's anything that links them, apart from dementia and extreme old age?'

She opened Alice's file and started reading it. Adams walked over to the desk and switched on the computer.

'You won't find much in those folders. Just original signatures, like the lasting powers of attorney. We can have a look at their online records if you like, but as we've written most of them, we already know what we'll find.'

He waited for the PC to boot up while his fiancée withdrew another folder, followed by two more. She compared them.

'What does "AHRL" mean?'

Adams shrugged.

'Most of the lawyers that drew up these powers of attorney have "Member of the AHRL" under their titles.'

The computer woke up and the doctor googled the acronym. 'Association of Human Rights Lawyers.'

They looked at each other. Tracy spoke.

'Why choose a human rights lawyer to draw up a basic legal document?' She pointed at the computer. 'Type "Alice Mansley human rights" and see what comes up.'

Adams read what appeared and grinned. 'Guess what? Our eldest centenarian was famous. "Dame arrested at Dounreay Power Station."' He clicked on the next result. '"Actress vows to fight on with Campaign for Nuclear Disarmament."' What the doctor saw under the third entry impressed him even more. 'Emmeline Pankhurst was her grandmother!'

'Really? You'd never have guessed from the way she talks – positively racist now.' Tracy felt she was on to something. 'Search "Brian Passen human rights".'

Adams wasn't quite so enamoured this time.

'"Company blames militant shop steward for factory closure."' The next reference to Brian appeared to surprise him. '"Union champions Passen as new Marx."' He looked up. 'I'd never have put Brian down as a communist.'

His future wife furrowed her brow. 'That's because we didn't know what he was like *before* he got Alzheimer's. Try "Gary Jacob human rights".'

The doctor seemed worried by what he found this time. '"Gangland thug jailed for life with no prospect of parole."' He checked some of the images with the result to make sure the news item detailed the exact same one-hundred and five-year-old Gary Jacob now residing in his ward. It unfortunately did. 'Drugs, prostitution, rape – you name it. So much for no parole – looks like those human rights lawyers managed to get him out.' A look of surprise appeared on his face. 'He's a murderer! I'm glad he seems to have changed his ways.'

Tracy pondered how stark the difference in him was. She selected another folder. 'Brian said Derek Bullingham assaulted him with his walking stick yesterday. I took Derek's side at the time because he was the most stressed about it, but he's always been a troublemaker.' She connected the dots from the search results and how the patients appeared now. 'I wonder if he was a diplomat or something like that before he got Alzheimer's?'

Adams placed his fingers on the keyboard, but then stopped. He sat back. 'It's the medication, Tracy. We both know how the red pill works. A dramatic change in personality is just another temporary side-effect that will eventually settle – no different to the thoughts of suicide. Well done for spotting it, though.'

Tracy thought he couldn't have been more patronising if he tried. 'So you knew about this?'

'No, I didn't, but wanting to commit suicide is just a bit more obvious than *not* wanting to rape and murder anymore, don't you think? Alzheimer's can cause some pretty extreme character changes, so think what the treatment has to do to combat that.'

His eyes settled on the computer's screen again. 'I wasn't aware of their *pre*-dementia conditions, though, and I must admit it does seem strange how different they are now.' He typed "Derek Bullingham human rights" into the address bar. He wasn't quite the B-list celebrity of the others, so it took a while to find him. The doctor chuckled when he did. 'You were nearly right.' He turned the screen so Tracy could see the image. It was of a priest.

She studied it. 'I can see the logic of the treatment turning the son of the Devil into an angel, but the other way around? That's a bit dangerous, isn't it? What if Derek tries to kill someone?'

Adams widened his eyes at her. 'Then he'll drop dead from the effort and justice will have been done.'

They stared at each other as an answer to Tracy's original question began to emerge. She offered what she was thinking.

'I wonder what Derek would be physically capable of now if he'd been a fifty-year-old early-onset dementia sufferer with no secondary conditions?'

The nurse counted the remaining folders. 'Including the poor man we've lost, there were originally fifteen patients. Let's see how many other saints have turned sinners and vice versa.'

The doctor sat back from the PC again. 'Aren't we making certain assumptions?'

'Like what?'

'That we're going to find them, for a start – they can't all have done something significant enough to be on the web.'

'Do as you're told!'

Adams sighed and entered the next name she gave him. He raised an eyebrow at how quickly he found his history, but took on a more serious air when the search results of the remaining ten patients appeared just as swiftly.

'Looks like we've found your link, Tracy – they've all done something worthy of a *Wikipedia* entry.' He mused on the significance of that. 'The professor must have wanted to compare their progress with their former selves. It makes sense, as none of them would have been able to recall it when they first arrived, and next of kin would only have known so much.' He looked up from the screen. 'A patient with either a famous or infamous background would be ideal in that regard.' He furrowed his brow. 'But why are we only finding this out now?'

Tracy finished writing. 'I make that eleven saints against four sinners.'

'But only three of them have criminal records?'

'One was a Tory MP.'

The doctor cocked his head to one side. 'I don't think being in the *nasty* party counts.'

She put her tongue in her cheek before sealing the patient's condemnation. 'And a man.'

Her beau jumped up and chased her around the office. He caught and tickled her just as the door opened.

Mike, the male nurse, looked at them both. Tracy glanced at her watch.

'Ooh – I'm late for my shift.'

She pushed Adams away and made for the exit. The two nurses grinned at each other and exchanged thumbs up as they left, gossiping.

'I guess our new social status is official after all.'

Adams looked at the notes Tracy had made and the two columns marked "Saints" and "Sinners" next to them. He chuckled at how readily she'd put the ex-Conservative Member of Parliament with the criminals, while the one ex-Labour MP they had on the clinical trial was apparently a good guy. *No need to guess which way my wife intends voting at the next general election then*, he thought to himself. He went to screw the page up when something else she'd written caught his eye. It was the words "Now a Nazi?" next to Alice's name.

Tracy had made a note of something she thought relevant next to most of the patients, and it caused the doctor to sit back down at the computer. He searched for Gary Jacob again and wrote down what he was hoping he wouldn't find. He did the same with the other two ex-cons on his ward. He sat back and pondered the meaning of what he'd discovered. 'Surely not?'

Adams turned to Tracy's saints and did the same. He ended up with a list of the patients' past allegiances and affiliations, which he wrote down in a distinct order – not in a list from top to bottom – but from left to right. It began with Alice's membership of the Campaign for Nuclear Disarmament and finished with Gary's association with the National Front.

Adams picked up what he'd written and stared at it in disbelief. Starting with the pacifists and communists on the left and finishing with the nationalists and fascists on the right, each patient appeared to represent a perfect example of a certain political or religious view. Or, rather, *did*. It wasn't just their personalities and characters that were different now – so were their individual social and theological beliefs. They were the opposite.

CHAPTER TWENTY

'Just so we can be absolutely clear, Sir John, the cure for Alzheimer's is one hundred per cent effective, but does still carry a small risk of suicide?'

Professor Savage looked away from Lady Amali and towards Alex Salib and Father Francis sitting in the public gallery. The distance between the two neither confirmed nor denied any collusion, although if they did have a hand in instigating this latest challenge to his work, it would have been for very different reasons. He studied the rest of the medical board to try and gauge his level of support, and then at the press gallery to speculate on what tomorrow's newspapers would have to say on the matter. He had hoped to make the results of the trial public at a time of his choosing, but that was impossible now. He answered the chairperson's question.

'The suicide side-effect has two distinct phases, Lady Amali. The first occurs a few weeks after surgery and around the time the new cells have become a physical part of the recipient's brain. The donor's own consciousness is then free to engage with the patient's, which, as you can imagine, can be somewhat troubling. Particularly with a dementia sufferer who hasn't been able to exercise their *own* consciousness for years, let alone have to accept someone else's. Under those circumstances, psychosis is all but inevitable, with hallucinations and extreme paranoia sadly leading to a desperation to want to end it all as soon as possible.'

Lady Amali looked down at what had been placed in front of her. 'On that point, Sir John, I see there have been a number of incidents during the clinical trial, some of which resulted in significant injury to the patients involved.'

She read out the report of Brian's accident with the barbecue. The professor concurred.

'We can't be absolutely certain, as no one witnessed him deliberately forcing his arm into the flames, but it does tie in with his suicidal thoughts at the time. The incident was recorded as being caused by the psychosis.'

Lady Amali nodded, as did some of the other board members. She motioned for Savage to continue.

'Fortunately, the medication has proven to be highly effective in combating these visions and fears, to the extent that every patient has now made a full recovery from their dementia.' He readied himself for the questions his next statement would generate. 'However, that success means all the patients are now able to understand the reality of their situation and that has led to a new phase of some considering *rational* suicide.'

The board members looked at each other and murmuring began amongst the public and press. Lady Amali banged her gavel.

'Sir John, are you saying the cure results in many of the patients still wanting to end their lives?'

The professor scanned the troubled faces of his supporters. 'First of all, I want to make it clear the treatment is *not* a cure. The new tissue acts as a surrogate in replacing the damaged cells – it doesn't terminate the disease which continues to exist. The introduced brain matter will suffer the exact same fate eventually, but hopefully not for many years. Secondly, although the procedure fully recovers a person's core competencies like physical movement, reasoning, judgement, and concentration, memory has been less successful. Only the ability to recognise family and a limited number of events from the past has had a positive outcome. Normal short and long-term memory only seem to begin functioning correctly again from mid-trial onwards. In essence, the further back in the past they look, the more they're able to recall, but much of it will have been *permanently* erased by the disease. I'm afraid in some cases that can mean decades of knowledge lost.'

Savage addressed the public and press. 'Imagine waking up one day totally conscious of the fact that you can no longer remember the last fifty years of your life – how do you think that would make you feel?'

The murmuring turned to louder chatter and he noticed the odd notes the press had been making became fevered. The gavel was banged again.

'Sir John, this isn't a presentation – it's an investigation – and I'd appreciate it if you would confine your comments to the board.'

Savage turned back and feigned a look of *mea culpa*. A fellow neurologist leaned across to whisper something in the chair's ear and she let him speak.

'Sir John, the trial has clearly produced some significant questions about your procedure. Why do you think the board should sanction your method for *all* dementia sufferers?' The professor noted more than a hint of professional jealousy in the voice.

He glanced at Alex and Father Francis. 'Because the benefits outweigh the risks. Six months ago, the last time any of the patients even recognised, let alone had a sensible conversation with, their loved ones, was at least five years previously.' He turned towards the public and press again. 'I fail to see how anyone could remain unmoved after witnessing such an emotional reunion.' He stood up. 'If you could have seen, as I have, the joy a simple pleasure that you and I take for gran—'

The gavel was banged once more. 'Sit down, Sir John! I won't tell you again.'

Savage capitulated with a gesture Uriah Heap would have been proud of. He mocked contrition. 'If I may continue?'

Lady Amali gave a single but stern nod of her head.

'Clear emotional benefits aside, quality of life has also been dramatically transformed. Again, six months ago, all of the trial patients were bedridden and completely unable to care for themselves or perform the simplest of tasks. They can now not only feed and dress with the minimum of assistance, but actively engage socially too. Indeed, if it were not for their secondary medical conditions, all would be perfectly capable of returning to whatever active life Alzheimer's had forced them to leave behind. Which brings me to my penultimate point.'

He went to stand again, but stopped as the chair raised the gavel and glared at him.

'Dementia currently costs the NHS and social services twenty-six billion pounds a year. Should the board sanction my procedure, that bill would be virtually eliminated within months.'

A louder conversation began and Lady Amali had to bang the gavel several times to bring the room to order. The hacks took out their mobile phones and tapped at them. The professor imagined the texts to be something like "Hold the front page".

'Sir John, are you seriously suggesting an extremely undesirable aspect of your treatment should be accepted just because it saves money?'

She had to bring the room to order again. Savage sensed a division opening amongst those present. They eventually settled.

'I'm suggesting the thoughts of suicide should be managed as part of normal palliative care – just as it is in any aged individual not having undergone the procedure. This is only an issue with the trial patients because they are all approaching the end of their normal lives anyway. Dementia is usually diagnosed some two to three decades earlier than this, so I would expect those sufferers to readily embrace their new selves. Without wishing to appear cold, once the current elderly generation is no longer with us, concerns with my treatment will cease.'

He saw his friend, Tarquin, wince as a member of the public shouted out: 'Yeah, just bury the mistakes.'

The heckler's comments set the public off again and the board used the noise as cover while they conferred for a few seconds. The chair brought the proceedings back under control.

'You said "penultimate"?'

Savage looked at Lady Amali and she repeated the question.

'You said: "which brings me to my penultimate point". So, what is your *final* point?'

Savage regarded the press again. He had intended to announce the successful transformation of the three notorious 1960s gangsters into what would now appear to be model citizens, but thought he'd said enough. No point in complicating matters at this stage. He glanced at Alex again before reneging on what he had promised he would say the day the treatment became public.

'Nothing. I must have been mistaken.'

Alex glared at him as someone shouted: 'Too right, mate. Who do you think you are? God?'

The medical board elected to adjourn until a later date and Lady Amali banged the gavel to end proceedings. The noise of it was lost in the melee that followed. She stood up to leave and the press surrounded the professor. He ignored their questions while ensuring the cameras caught his best side. There was a parting of the waves as Alex forced her wheelchair through the throng until she was within earshot.

'Coward!'

She spun round to barge her way back out again. It was the chaplain's turn next.

'You lied to God, Sir John, and he won't forget that!' He followed Alex out of the room.

The press left when they thought they had everything they were going to get and Tarquin approached. 'So, how do you think the papers will view you tomorrow, eh, John? My guess is page three of the broadsheets, but the front pages of the red-tops, will split you firmly fifty~fifty – hero on the right, villain of the piece on the left.' He seemed to think he knew why the surgeon's popularity wasn't greater. 'When are you going to learn that saying things like "without wishing to appear cold" makes you look like the iceberg that sank the *Titanic*?'

Savage closed his briefcase and gave his friend a look that was just as frozen. 'The gentlemen of the press will make of this what they will, but you and I both know it will boil down to the politics of the money – is an annual saving of twenty-six billion pounds worth putting up with the embarrassment of a few old dears packing their bags for Switzerland? Or, as our cerebrally challenged friend unwittingly grunted earlier, can any mistakes be both literally and metaphorically buried by other bad news?'

Tarquin lowered his voice. 'I'm glad you decided not to mention the separate success with the less desirable characters on your trial. Recovering someone's mind is one thing, but deliberately manipulating it is quite another.'

The eminent neurologist smiled at the Business Secretary. 'Money will still talk, Tarquin.'

CHAPTER TWENTY-ONE

'So, how are my lab rats coming along?'

The doctor had always assumed Professor Savage was joking whenever he said that, but he wasn't so sure now. That morning's newspapers lay on the professor's desk and Savage featured prominently on the front pages of most of them. Headlines like 'HEARTLESS!' and 'BREAKTHROUGH!' predominated.

Adams updated him on the patients' progress. 'They've all now accepted their new selves. The pre-existing secondary conditions and thoughts of so-called rational suicide are the only remaining issues.'

The nation's newest love~hate figure smiled. 'And Cecil?'

The doctor skewed his head to one side. 'Don't you mean Mr Passen?'

'Oh, yes – my apologies. Force of habit.'

The doctor's concerns with the professor's ethics increased. 'I've told his family the end of the week, but I'll be surprised if he's still with us tomorrow morning.'

His superior took in the front page of the *Morning Star*. It was the only paper that didn't have a picture of him – the Green Party's newest MP occupied it instead. Savage passed comment.

'Not the most flattering of news items, I'm afraid. Ms Salib seems determined to get her way. You'd think she'd be grateful for a chance to resurrect her beloved Voluntary Euthanasia Bill.' He looked back up at the doctor. 'We can't keep relying on the Swiss to do it for us.'

Adams used the mention of euthanasia as an excuse to raise what was troubling him. 'Sir John, I take it we can be confident that a patient electing to engage with an organisation like Dignitas is genuinely doing so of their own *free* will?'

An uncomfortable silence followed. The professor offered him a seat.

'My dear chap, something appears to be troubling you. How can I be of help?'

Adams sat down. 'The newspapers refer to the second phase of suicidal thoughts as a side-effect, but I'm not so sure it is.'

Savage leaned back in his chair, made a steeple out of his fingers and placed them under his chin. 'Tell me. What has led you to come to such a disturbing notion?'

The doctor explained his concern. 'We've always known the trial would result in the test subjects having at least *some* of the personality traits of the donor but, rather than producing a kind of hybrid, it's clear an entirely *new* character has emerged in each of them.'

'Really, Doctor, I'm surprised. You of all people should know how unpredictable the field of neurology is.'

'That's my point, Sir John. It appears to be anything but.'

Another embarrassing silence followed. The professor invited his colleague to go on.

'The trial drug was designed to meld the two minds together, so we've reported all physical and psychological recovery as progress. However, that was only because it was measured against our understanding of what constitutes normal behaviour – recognition of family members, able to feed oneself, make decisions, etcetera. But when their pre-dementia lives are factored in, a very different and, I have to say, *perturbing* pattern emerges.'

The professor looked at his aquarium while the doctor elaborated.

'It would appear that any political or religious affinity held in the past has not just changed, but been completely *reversed* in the process.'

Savage got up and walked over to the tank. The doctor followed him.

'Sir John, the patients' previous interests and beliefs weren't just casual – they were all individually active in their chosen fields and together formed a broad spectrum of nearly every social or theological belief in society. Which is too much of a coincidence for them *not* to have been chosen for those reasons alone.' He readied himself for the accusation he was about to make. 'Sir John, did you *deliberately* select the test subjects because you not only wanted to treat their dementia, but the *way* they thought, too?'

Savage studied his specimens. Two Siamese fighting

fish entered a short tussle with each other and he grinned. He turned to face the doctor and dropped the smile.

'I'm not interested in treating dementia.'

The words stunned Adams. Savage didn't seem to be in the least bit concerned with the ethical implications of what he'd just said. His next statement was no less disturbing.

'Did you know goldfish only have a memory of a few seconds? It's nonsense, of course, a bit like an elephant never forgetting, but the one thing I have always admired about the less cerebral passengers on this planet is that they never use violence or coercion for religious, political, or ideological reasons – just survival.' He stared at his fish taking the occasional swipe at each other. 'Imagine if people could be made to think the same way.'

Adams took a couple of steps back from the man he thought he knew. 'Sir John, whatever wider application you think the treatment for Alzheimer's has to offer, society will never accept artificial manipulation of a person's beliefs, no matter what the benefit.'

The professor recovered his smile and seemed to change the subject. 'I hear congratulations are in order! Finally – a chance to open the Glenmorangie!'

He strode over to the drinks cabinet, the sudden change of tone catching the doctor off-guard for a moment.

'I'm sorry, Sir John, but I'm going to have to report this.'

Savage pulled the doors of the cabinet open and

reached for two glasses. 'No need; I did that some weeks ago.'

Adams frowned. 'To whom?'

'Those who need to know – GMC, NICE, Health Secretary, Home Secretary, opposition parties, that sort of level.'

The frown turned to puzzlement. 'What was their response?'

The whisky was uncorked and the aroma savoured. 'Same as you, of course – complete and utter horror. Especially poor Ms Salib.'

The doctor looked at Alex's picture on the front page of the *Morning Star*. 'You told *her*? A far-left politician?'

The professor offered him a glass. 'Perhaps you would have preferred I just inform the incumbent *right*-wing government how best to ensure its citizens conform to their way of thinking?'

The doctor took the whisky. 'No, but…'

'Congratulations! Here's to the happy couple.'

The glasses clinked but Adams couldn't summon any enthusiasm, managing only a weak, 'Thank you.'

The professor closed his eyes. 'Strange how love can completely alter one's mind.' He opened them again and looked at the doctor's forehead. 'One minute a carefree bachelor, the next an obedient husband.'

Adams scoffed at the implied analogy. 'There's a huge difference between nature's subtle persuasions and direct interference, Professor.'

Savage nodded. 'Oh, I agree. Which is why I thought it best to allow our elected peers to choose the way forward. After all, in the wrong hands, the treatment could be extremely dangerous.'

The doctor became agitated. 'The *way forward* is obvious – it has to be made illegal.'

'Oh, come now, Doctor. It's no different to any other medical discovery. It just needs to be applied correctly.'

Adams put down his glass. 'Applied *correctly*? Is that what you call changing a founding member of CND into a Nazi? *Correcting* her?'

Savage poured himself another whisky. 'Alice is over one hundred years old. She's hardly likely to start the Fourth Reich. And, anyway, as a psychologist I'm sure even you can appreciate my need to explore the possibilities to their *fullest* extent.' He walked back over to the doctor. 'Strange how I don't hear you protesting about the National Front fascist thug turned pacifist?'

Adams fumbled his reply. 'Well, that's different.'

'Is it really? What were the words you used just now? "Society will never accept artificial manipulation of a person's beliefs no matter what the benefit."'

The doctor felt he was being manipulated himself in some way.

The professor appeared to sympathise with his predicament. 'Don't worry, Doctor. The government feels exactly the same, which is why they wish to proceed with a new trial featuring some of the many unfortunates currently residing at Her Majesty's pleasure.' He picked up the doctor's glass and offered it back to him. 'I wonder what menagerie of miscreants our lords and potential masters will select? The far-right will predictably want some wretched but indigenous Afro-Caribbean made to think he or she should return to the birthplace of their ancestors, whereas Ms Salib will be equally boring in insisting some billionaire jailed for corruption is encouraged to give all his money away. The democratic process should result in the attendance of young Muslim fundamentalists requiring deradicalisation, but the realist in me thinks we'll probably end up turning yet more white male middle-class rapists and murderers into everyone's favourite uncle. How dull.'

The doctor ignored his glass. 'No matter how sensible turning a convicted criminal into a law-abiding citizen sounds, it's still brainwashing and the public won't accept it.'

Savage placed both glasses on his desk and sat down at it. 'I told the medical board yesterday that if it sanctions the treatment for Alzheimer's disease, the taxpayer will save twenty-six billion pounds almost overnight. Do you know how much would be saved if all the prisons were to close?'

Adams didn't respond.

'More than twice that.'

The doctor started to say something but the professor interrupted him.

'And that's just the post-conviction costs. Imagine if pre-conviction was made a thing of the past too? What if the law courts, prosecution services, probation...?' He stood up again. 'Even the *police* were no longer required?'

Savage paused to look at the two fighting fish squaring up to each other again. 'What do you think your precious *public* would make of no more theft, no more rape, and no more murder?' He narrowed his eyes at the doctor. 'What do you think they would make of no more *war*?'

Adams tried to reason with him. 'Professor, as a psychologist, of course I'm professionally interested to see if the treatment could be altruistically applied elsewhere, but just as prefrontal lobotomy was once accepted and then utterly discredited as a means to control mental illness, so will this be. It's just too short a step to a dystopian society of blind obedience. The world won't accept it.'

The professor sighed. 'If I'd told you a year ago I intended conducting surgery on fifteen fit and healthy young men and women just so I could prove their politics could be reversed, would you have even allowed it to happen, let alone become involved?'

The doctor didn't answer.

'So I decided to make it more palatable for everyone by choosing fifteen decrepit geriatrics and presenting it as a treatment for dementia instead.' He held up two of the most favourable tabloids. 'Incredible thing the human brain, Doctor. Even non-intrusive methods of brainwashing can be highly effective at getting one's own way. Just ask Nurse Roberts.'

Adams became angry. 'You didn't answer my question – are the patients' thoughts of suicide *truly* their own?'

Savage grinned. 'All lab rats end up in the furnace, James.'

To be continued…

EPILOGUE

Brian ran his fingers through Claire's hair and cupped her face with his hands. 'Oh, darling, it's so wonderful to see you again. I've missed you so much.' He kissed her on the lips before sitting back and trying to take in as much of her as he could. He couldn't. He was just so happy. Happier than he'd ever been. 'Am I dead?'

Claire smiled and nodded.

'So, is this *Heaven*?'

She nodded again.

'Oh, I think I may have been a bit rude to, er, God.'

He glanced around as if expecting to be struck down at any second. His wife laughed at him.

'Don't worry, Brian. I'm sure he'll forgive you.'

'So, he does exist then?'

'Beats me. I've never seen him.' She pulled him close and buried her head in his chest.

The feeling of being back together at last was pure bliss. Brian looked up to see the sun poking its rays through the trees in the garden. There was something soft between his bare toes – it was grass intermixed with wild flowers. The sound of giggling made him realise he wasn't only back with Claire – the whole family were together again. The scene just needed the smell of a barbecue and the flight of a single bumble bee and everything would be perfect. It was.

He brought his wife's face up to meet his. 'So, what do we do in this eternal paradise?'

She raised her eyebrows at him. 'I'm sure you'll think of something.'

He pursed his lips. 'Much as we have a lot of catching-up to do in *that* department, even I can't imagine doing it forever. Think of our backs.'

Claire laughed. 'It's Heaven, Brian. No more health issues, no more money problems, worrying what the future holds – in fact, no more concerns at all. Just happiness – forever.'

Their daughter ran over and tried to wrap her arms around the two of them. She and Brian grinned at each other.

'Looks like you can dream of Heaven too. I can't imagine Lucy actually wanting to be a six-year-old again.' He turned back to his wife. 'Which means you're probably not real either.'

Claire rested her head on his chest. 'Does it matter?'

Brian took in the unmistakable aroma of her hair and ran his hand through Lucy's. 'No. It's the perfect dream and I never want to wake up from it.'

Lucy seemed to tease him. 'Come on, Daddy – wake up!'

'Wake up!' She had a man's voice, suddenly. 'Wake up, Cecil.'

Someone took hold of his hand. His wife, daughter, garden – all were gone.

It was dark.

'Can you hear me?'

A man.

Brian's left hand was being shaken. He opened his eyes.

Not dead. Not in Heaven. No longer in the perfect dream. A steady beeping sound could be heard and he started to cry.

'Do you recognise me?'

Brian squinted in the direction of Professor Savage's voice. The difference between reality and the dream was unbearable.

'I just want to die, Professor.' It hurt, but he gripped the unwelcome visitor's hand as hard as he could. *'Please.'*

'Don't worry, old chap. All in good time. There's something I need to check first.'

Savage held up what appeared to be a pair of 3D virtual reality glasses. Brian looked at them through his tears in disbelief.

'You woke me from my perfect dream to play some stupid game?'

Savage tried to reassure him. 'It's just a sleep mask. It's important not to be distracted by any light.'

Brian wanted to become angry, but he was too weak. 'Then what?'

'Then I'll ask you a few questions and that will be it.'

'I can tell you my name and the year just as easily with my eyes closed.'

'They won't be the questions. And I need you to perform a few simple tasks too – indulge me for a few moments, if you will.'

Brian turned his attention to the machine making the monotonous sound. The rate of it picked up. 'And what will you do for *me* in return?'

Savage looked at the heart monitor too. 'Whatever is within my power.'

The machine settled down again.

'Will Claire and I be together?'

The professor sighed. 'Not if your treatment is anything to go by, I'm afraid. You clearly needed physical brain matter to remember her again and I don't think Heaven allows that.' He studied the deteriorating vital signs. 'I can help you get back to your dream, though?'

Brian was hardly in a position to argue. 'Okay. But be warned, any fairground rides and I'll just be sick on you.'

Savage raised the top third of the bed and slipped the soft cotton blindfold over Brian's head. 'Comfortable?'

Brian nodded. Something cold was then placed against his temple. It caused him to become nauseous and a few seconds later, he vomited. The rate of beeping increased. He tried removing the mask but the professor wouldn't let him.

Brian was stressed. 'I warned you. I didn't even see anything that time.'

The beats per minute of the heart monitor reduced – along with the professor's concern. Brian tried once more to remove the blindfold, but a hand stopped him again. He was too weak to fight and, if anything, the retching had made him weaker.

'Terribly sorry about that, old chap, but I was afraid you'd refuse if I said you were going to vomit anyway. I just need you to assist me for a few minutes more and then we'll be done. Let me know when you're ready.'

Brian's heart might have been diseased but his cynicism was still healthy. 'How unusual. A medic keen to keep me in the dark – literally, this time.'

His nausea passed. 'Okay, Professor – I'm ready.'

'What can you see?'

Brian shrugged. 'I'm wearing a mask doing a pretty good job of keeping all the light out – just blackness. Oh, wait a minute. There's a white dot – down on the right.'

'Good. I want you to look at it.'

A moment later and the dot had moved to the centre of Brian's vision.

'Ooh. Now it's right in front of me. How did you do that?'

'Now bring it towards you.'

Brian raised a hand to grab it, but felt his arm being pulled back down to the bed again.

'It's not physical. You need to *think* it closer.'

Brian was just about to ask what the professor meant by that when the blackness became a bright light.

'That's too much – pull back or push it away.'

The bright light went back to being a white dot, then another bright light, before Brian got the hang of what he was supposed to be doing. The home page of the hospital's website filled his vision. He groaned.

'Another bloody portable television.'

He pulled the sleep mask off. The web page stayed where it was. Brian closed his eyes, but it was still there. He panicked and the heart monitor's alarm went off.

'It won't go away! Make it go away!'

The professor grabbed him. 'Stay calm. Move your eyes rapidly in any direction.'

Fear made Brian do that anyway. The web page reduced to a small white dot somewhere in the lower right periphery of his vision. The crash team burst through the door just as Brian's anxiety had started to reduce. Savage waved them away. The alarm ceased of its own accord and the team left the room.

'*That* was just about my worst nightmare. I *hate* modern technology.' Brian pointed towards his iPad. 'That thing's bad enough, but at least it's got something on it worth seeing.' He smiled at the current image of his wife, but then tutted as it rolled over to the next. 'See?'

Savage picked up the tablet, tapped the screen a couple of times, and then introduced his phone to one of the edges. He turned the iPad back towards its owner. The screen was now black save for a small white dot in the bottom right-hand corner of it.

Brian harrumphed. He glanced at the dot in his own field of view and scoffed again. Curiosity got the better of him and he was soon not just seeing but controlling his favourite images of Claire – just by thinking about them. He smiled as he was finally able to view her photographs in any order and for however long he wanted.

'This is more like it – much more sensible. What did you call this?'

Savage checked the vital signs again. 'Augmented consciousness. It enables the user of an electronic device to operate it by thought alone. Should do very well when it's made available to the public next year.'

Brian produced the eye movements necessary to reduce the visions back to a dot.

'Device?'

The professor thought for a moment. 'Portable televisions.'

His guinea pig looked at him. 'But won't they have to go through some kind of brain surgery first?'

Savage grinned and widened his eyes. 'Oh, yes.'

Brian went back to the photograph album. He decided to settle on a black and white studio portrait of his family – taken some time around the mid-sixties, judging by the length of the skirts. Tears were soon flowing freely again. He searched for the professor's hand and grabbed it.

'*Please*. Do it *now*.'

Savage began keeping to his side of the agreement. He disabled the heart monitor's alarm.

The smartphone was placed against Brian's temple again. Within a few seconds, Brian's eyelids flickered, as did the iPad image of his family. The vital signs on the monitor reduced. Brian closed his eyes for the last time and the screen on the iPad went black with just the white dot visible in the bottom right-hand corner of it. The phone began displaying the neural activity the professor was looking for – all signs indicated Brian Passen would be breathing his last in the next minute or so.

Savage let go of Brian's hand. The fingers were turning blue. Brian's breathing became more erratic as the professor continued to hold the smartphone in position while alternating his attention between it and the closed eyes. He was waiting for something to happen and, if it didn't in the next few seconds, it never would.

'Come on, old chap. You can do it.'

Brian's eyes twitched under their lids, which corresponded to an increase in activity on the phone. Savage began transferring Brian's subconscious to the hospital's mainframe.

What looked to be lights flashed across the screen of the iPad. The vital signs on the heart monitor flatlined, and the professor noted the time of death once he was sure Brian was no longer breathing and his heart had stopped. The now decaying brain activity was still being transferred, though it would all be white noise unless coherent dreaming began, and that was something the professor had yet to fully understand, let alone gain control of.

The flashing lights on the iPad morphed into an image and Savage breathed a sigh of relief. It was of a garden. There was a barbecue and the woman and child standing next to it ran towards the observer.

It took another minute for the professor to be satisfied with everything he came for, but he continued to hold his phone against the head of the cadaver until all the neural activity in it had ceased. Savage then disabled the link to the iPad, but not before confirming Brian appeared to be pleased with the outcome of his trial too.

Savage pondered how best to ensure the authorities would allow a person's consciousness to remain active after death. The condition would help ease the acceptance of compulsory euthanasia politically, but convincing the clergy would be more of a challenge.

He bent down to his lab rat and kissed it on the forehead. 'Sweet dreams, Cecil.'

BOOK TWO

CONDITION

THE CURING BEGINS...

ALEC BIRRI

CONDITION

BOOK TWO

THE CURING BEGINS...

Discovering an infamous Nazi doctor conducted abortions in Argentina after the Second World War may not come as a surprise, but why was the twisted eugenicist not only allowed to continue his evil experiments but encouraged to do so? And what has that got to do with a respected neurologist in 2027? Surely the invention of a cure for nearly all the world's ailments can't possibly have its roots buried in the horrors of Auschwitz?

The unacceptable is about to become the disturbingly bizarre. What has the treatment's 'correction' of paedophiles got to do with the President of the United States, the Pope, and even the UK's Green Party?

As if the CONDITION trilogy wasn't unsettling enough.

10 $\frac{99}{}$

RECEIVED JUL 2 0 2017

9 781785 899683